AF009

MASSIMILIANO AFIERO

AXIS FORCES 9

WW2 AXIS FORCES

The Axis Forces 009 - First edition February 2019 by Luca Cristini Editor for the brand Soldiershop
Cover & Art Design by soldiershop factory.   ISBN code: 978-88-93274234
Copyright © 2019 Luca Cristini Editore (BG) ITALY.   No part of this publication may be reproduced, stored in a retrieval system or transmitted by any form or by any means, electronic, recording or otherwise without the prior permission in writing from the publishers. The publisher remains to disposition of the possible having right for all the doubtful sources images or not identifies.
Visit www.soldiershop.com to read more about all our books and to buy them.

The Axis Forces number 9 – February 2019

Direction and editing
Via San Giorgio, 11 – 80021 AFRAGOLA (NA) - ITALIA
Managing and Chief Editor: Massimiliano Afiero
Email: maxafiero@libero.it - **Website**: www.maxafiero.it

Contributors
Stefano Canavassi, Carlos Caballero Jurado, Rene Chavez, Carlo Cucut, Daniel Fanni, Dmitry Frolov, Antonio Guerra, John B. Köser, Lars Larsen, Christophe Leguérandais, Eduardo M. Gil Martínez, Peter Mooney, Péter Mujzer, Ken Niewiarowicz, Erik Norling, Raphael Riccio, Marc Rikmenspoel, Charles Trang, Cesare Veronesi, Sergio Volpe

Editorial

With this issue we begin our third year of publication of our and your military history magazine dedicated to Axis military formations during the Second World War. Thanks to the wide circulation of the magazine all over the world, we are receiving many compliments and appreciations for the work done so far, but our intent is to continue to improve and offer you new and unpublished historical research. Critics have come, of course, some readers have complained about our bad English in some articles. We apologize for this, but consider that most of our contributors are not native English speakers and their articles come to us in their original language. We still need to improve our translation work. We are always grateful to everyone for their cooperation. Let's now analyze the contents of this issue of the magazine. Let's start with the second part of the article dedicated to the Dutch Legion, *richly illustrated. We continue with the biography of Zvonimir Bernwald, at first a volunteer in the* Handschar *Division and then in the 31st SS Division. It continues with the third part of the article dedicated to the* Barbarigo *battalion on the Anzio front, with a new excerpt from the new book by Tomasz Borowski on the last combat actions of the French volunteers of* Charlemagne, *the fourth and final part of the photographic report dedicated to the SS-Hauptsturmführer Hans-Jörg Hartmann and we close with a long and comprehensive article on Romanian armored formations. Happy reading to everyone and see you in the next issue.*

Massimiliano Afiero

The publication of The Axis Forces deals exclusively with subjects of a historical military nature and is not intended to promote any type of political ideology either present or past, as it also does not seek to exalt any type of political regime of the past century or any form of racism.

Contents

The Dutch Volunteer Legion, 2nd part	Pag. 5
Zvonimir Bernwald, 13. SS-Division 'Handschar' and 31. SS-Division	Pag. 15
The Barbarigo Battalion on the Anzio front, 3rd part	Pag. 23
The last battle of the Charlemagne Division, 2nd part	Pag. 32
SS-Hauptsturmfuhrer Hans-Jörg Hartmann, 4th part	Pag. 43
Romanian Armored Forces in World War II	Pag. 53

The Dutch Volunteer Legion
by Massimiliano Afiero – 2nd part

A 7,5 cm Pak40 on a defensive position.

Destroyed Russian tanks.

Under enemy fire....

New enemy attacks

On 10 February 1943, the Soviets launched a surprise attack without any preparatory artillery fire. Mooyman quickly opened fire, while the German infantry, exhausted after days of uninterrupted combat, retreated in great disorder. The Dutch volunteers ran to their aid, convincing them to return to their positions. Meanwhile Mooyman had continued to do his duty; First Gunner Buttinger had by himself managed to destroy a Soviet anti-tank gun in an intrepid action. After having been able to get close to the Soviet position without being detected, at about twenty meters from the enemy position he cut down all of the gunners. The Bolshevik attack was finally stopped just a few meters short of the main defensive line. That evening, Mooyman was presented with the Iron Cross First Class while the hero of the day, Buttinger, was awarded the Second Class. During the night, it began to snow heavily. The countryside became covered completely in white. Mooyman remained at his post, heedless of the snow that was falling. When the relief squad appeared, he was found covered with snow up to his nose. Two hours later, some cannon fire was heard.

Kooper, a Dutch medical aide, fired a white flare into the air to illuminate the area, thus revealing that the Soviets had emplaced an anti-tank gun along the railway line. Mooyman quicjly got it in his sights and gave the order to fire. The resulting shot managed only to drive off the crew, as the gun itself was in a defilade position and was impossible to hit with direct fire. What could be done?

A German anti-tank gun (7,5 cm *Pak40*) ready to fire on the Leningrad Front.

Gerardus Mooyman.

At about thirty or forty meters from the gun the Soviets had placed some lookouts in the hulk of one of their knocked out tanks. Those enemy observers had to be eliminated at all costs. From the other side of the railroad embankment the Soviets could be heard yelling and screaming. Could this be the beginning of a new attack, asked Erklenz. *"..Don't be foolish, they're only drunk, let's move"* replied Mooyman. At that moment, the young Dutch volunteer showed his wits and his ability to make a quick decision. His sole intention was to eliminate the dangerous enemy anti-tank gun. Volunteers Kooper and Hissink followed him. The three of them advanced with the greatest caution towards the enemy position. Then Mooyman left the other two behind to cover him. He then reached the enemy gun and placed a 3 kg explosive charge under the gun. When the explosion blew the Soviet gun to bits, the trio had already returned to their position without incurring any wounds.

Soviet light tank *T-60* with troops on the march.

A German Pak Camouflaged and ready for action.

Dutch Volunteers on the Leningrad Front, 1943.

On the morning of 13 February, the Soviets resumed their attack with tanks. The Dutch anti-tank guns, however, were still in place. Four Soviet tanks were destroyed and another two were damaged. But Mooyman was once again left without any ammunition; the platoon leader arrived just as five Soviet tanks were drawing perilously close. He gave the order to fire the last armor piercing round against the lead enemy tank and to fire high explosive rounds against the others. But Mooyman didn't want to admit to being beaten, and with Feldt's assistance, was able to get some fresh ammunition. Gunner Bouts, further to the north with his gun, still had a good supply on hand as his sector had been quiet. *SS-Sturmmann* Fekter, a young Hungarian volunteer who was an excellent harmonica player, carried the ammunition while under Soviet fire. Mooyman's gun resumed firing and two Soviet tanks were knocked out. Meanwhile the gap that had been opened in the main defensive line had been plugged, and without tank support the Soviet infantry chose to withdraw. Around 11:00, about twenty Soviet tanks returned to attack, heading towards the position occupied by Bouts. About eight hundred meters from his position, however, the tanks abruptly changed direction, once again heading for Mooyman's position. Luckily, the Dutch *Sturmmann* had been resupplied well, which enabled him to fire against the enemy at a furious rate. Six of the twenty Soviet tanks went up in flames, one after another. Still other tanks were hit and damaged, and the rest opted to turn around. Mooyman had won once again. It was then Bouts' turn to suffer a new tank attack; the untiring Fekter managed to get a few rounds to him in time. Bouts destroyed three tanks, but could have done more if he had had more ammunition.

A German anti-tank gun in a Russian village on the Leningrad Front, February 1943.

Dutch SS Volunteers moving a Gun.

He was in somewhat of a rage because he had given up his own ammunition to supply the other guns. Mooyman had been firing for the whole day and he had to let several enemy tanks get away without being able to do anything about it. Närger no longer had any enemy tanks within sight, as Mooyman had already dispatched all of them. The last rounds fired by Bouts fell at the moment that the German counterattack began. The reserves had arrived; they were grenadiers from a German division to the north. Stupefied, the Dutchmen watched this marvelous battalion advance, in close ranks, with their major leading them. The *Wehrmachtsbericht* of 13 February 1943, emphasized the heroism of the Dutch volunteers: "...*The Dutch volunteers played an important role in stopping the Bolshevik attack* south of Lake Ladoga, protecting the flank with their anti-tank guns. The most courageous Dutch gunner, who destroyed thirteen enemy armored vehicles, was SS-Mann *Gerardus Mooyman*".

The Knight's Cross for Mooyman

Gerardus Mooyman (on the right), is putting stripes on the barrel of his anti-tank gun, February 1943.

German defensive position with an *MG-34*, 1943.

An anti-tank gun in combat against Russian tanks.

At the end of the day the accounts were tallied: the Dutch *Panzerjägers* had destroyed fifteen tanks, thirteen for Mooyman and two for Bouts. That night *Generalleutnant* Erwin Sander, commander of *170.Infanterie Division*, wrote up a citation for Mooyman for the award of the Knight's Cross. The young Dutch *Sturmmann* had fired against the Soviet tanks as though he had been in a shooting gallery, with odds of 1 against 10. The proposal was also warmly endorsed by *SS-Brigadeführer* Fritz von Scholz, commander of the 2nd SS Infantry Brigade. The next day the Soviets attacked again, and Mooyman destroyed another three enemy tanks. He painted the twentieth white ring on the barrel of his gun, signifying twenty enemy tank kills. Stories of Mooyman's success began to make the rounds at the front and the Brigade received a message of congratulations from the OKW. There was also talk of the Dutch *Panzerjäger* on German radio.

Quite suddenly the presence of Dutch volunteers on the Leningrad front was noticed by everyone. Mooyman himself would later say: "...*Our jaws dropped when all of a sudden we saw a large group of officials who came to visit our positions and our anti-tank gun...*". But not all of the Dutch anti-tank guns were as lucky as was Mooyman's. On 15 February 1943, the *Pak* commanded by *SS-Rottenführer* Kosbau was hit by Soviet artillery fire after having fired only a few rounds. *SS-Sturmmannn* Wituschek, Diner and de Wit were killed outright. The sense of comradeship was however stronger than death itself and that night, *SS-Sturmmann* Närger received orders to retrieve the bodies of his fallen comrades. Närger left soon thereafter; it was a difficult task, and many preferred to face death rather than to touch a copse. But a sentiment of indissoluble solidarity prevailed at the front, based upon a shared sacrifice. During his difficult trip along the trace of the old main defensive line, Närger met many German units that were pulling back.

German defensive position with an anti-tank gun, Leningrad Front.

Dutch volunteers.

A destroyed Russian tank (*T-34*), February 1943.

The German infantrymen asked Närger where he was headed, but he limited his answer to saluting them. After a while he finally reached the destroyed gun and luckily for him, just at that moment a German truck happened to be passing by, which was ideal for towing the anti-tank gun and the bodies of his comrades. Legionnaire de Wit, who had been seventeen years old, was so light that Närger needed no effort to take him in his arms and place him on the vehicle. The lifeless bodies of Dinter and Wituschek turned out to be somewhat heavier...

The Dutch anti-tank company was able to deploy only four anti-tank guns along the new front line. During the three days that followed, the Soviets sent out only reconnaissance patrols and limited themselves to shelling German positions with their artillery. During one attack, *Sturmmannn* Buttinger and Ruiter were seriously wounded; they both died shortly after in a hospital from the wounds they had sustained. Bouts and Mooyman took advantage of a brief respite in the fighting to arrange for a "*Russian style*" resupply effort, looting the knocked out Soviet tanks; although the Soviet infantry may have had nothing more than a few kernels of corn and some raw fish their its knapsacks, the tankers were much better supplied.

In a trench with Soviet prisoners, February 1943.

More decorations arrived for the Dutch anti-tank gunners in those days; the Iron Cross First Class for Feldt and for the tireless aid man Kooper, while the Iron Cross Second Class was awarded to Bouts, Fekter, van der Wey, Benzinger, Wolferen, Waardenburg and Hissing. Almost all of the crews of Bouts and Mooyman received decorations.

The battle continues

The Soviets needed four days to reorganize and to return on the attack in the Schlüsselburg corridor. On the morning of 22 February, a tempest of fire fell upon the German positions. The crews of the Paks of Bouts and Mooyman stayed in their bunkers to listen to the *"concert"*. It was a veritable hell. The lookout suddenly gave the alarm: *"...Three tanks, back there, in the forest!"*. This time it looked like the end was at hand. The enemy tanks had come very close to the Dutch positions. Fortunately, the anti-tank guns had been well revetted and camouflaged. Mooyman ran between his men and the tanks, galloping along towards his gun that was about 150 meters away. Once he reached the position, he realized that there were five tanks advancing towards him. He gave a quick glance to Bouts, who had also joined his men, and he swung into action. The *Pak* with the twenty white kill rings on its barrel was swung around 180°, which certainly was not child's play given the weight of the gun and the frigid temperature. Then he began like a

Mooyman with the Knight's Cross.

madman to fire against the enemy tanks; two were hit immediately, but a third was missed. Bouts was luckier this time, managing to knock out three tanks. Once again the Dutch *Panzerjägers* had repulsed a Soviet armored attack; enthusiastic over their success, the Dutch volunteers began to inspect the destroyed tanks, oblivious of the danger of ambush. Soviet artillery had in fact begun to shell their positions, which had been spotted during their duel against the tanks, with violent fire.

Gerardus Mooyman seen here on the cover of the popular *Hamburger Illustrierte*.

Gerardus Mooyman with the Knight's Cross.

The *Pak* belonging to Bouts was the first to take a direct hit; a cloud of smoke wreathed the position. Mooyman was the first to run to the scene to see what had happened to his mates. Bouts fell in his arms, his uniform full of blood. *"Everyone else is dead, the gun is done for"* he said with a trembling voice. Van der Wey, Arts and Fekter had fallen on the field of honor. Mooyman turned to Bouts: *"..Your wound isn't serious, let's go look at the gun"*. The sights were ruined and one wheel was sheared off cleanly; for the time being the gun was out of action. Mooyman and Bouts then went to Mooyman's gun. When they got there all of the crew were gathered around Hissink, who had been wounded in the arm. After having been patched up as best as conditions would allow, Hissink was sent to the aid station, while Bouts wanted to stay where he was, requesting to take the place of Hissink in Mooyman's anti-tank gun crew. This was the last combat action for the Dutch on the Neva front. Two days later the order came to withdraw towards the Mga River. Bouts was awarded the Iron Cross First Class.

The Knight's Cross

When the Dutch volunteers reached the railway station at Mga, as they were waiting for the train, a motorcycle messenger arrived at full speed. *"Where is Mooyman"* he shouted. The young Dutch *Sturmmannn* stepped forward. *"Tomorrow you have to report to the 28.Jäger-Division command post, understood?"*. *"Yes, but what do they want with me?"* replied Mooyman, horrified. The courier departed without another word. On 26 February 1943, *SS-Sturmmannn* Gerardus Mooyman, nineteen years old, mechanic's apprentice, stood at attention in front of a guard of honor that saluted him. *General der Artillerie* Johann Sinhuber, commanding the German *28.Jäger-Division*, drew close and awarded him the Knight's Cross.

Mooyman receiving congratulations by *SS-Brigdf.* von Scholz, commander of *2.SS.Inf.Brigade*.

Mooyman with the Knight's Cross around his neck.

The scene was filmed by operators from the newsreel *"Die Deutsche Wochenschau"*, and was shown in movie theaters throughout half of Europe. Mooyman was the very first non-German European volunteer to be awarded the Knight's Cross. From that moment on his comrades took to jokingly calling him *"der Panzerjäger"* (the Tank Destroyer). His epic story was published in many newspapers and magazines. Himmler personally congratulated him, inviting him to participate in many ceremonies and parades held in his honor. When he returned to Holland, after having been given a period of leave as a reward, he was welcomed with all honors by his countrymen.

Mooyman at a meeting with head of the NSB, Mussert.

Return of Dutch legionnaires to Holland, 1943.

Mooyman continued his military career first in the *Nederland* Brigade and then in the *Nederland* Division. After having been promoted to the ranks of *Rottenführer* and then *Unterscharführer*, in early 1944 he attended an officer's course, graduating in June of that year with the rank of *Untersturmführer*. His activity as an anti-tank officer continued until the end of the war in *SS-Panzerjäger Abteilung* 23 of the SS *Nederland* Division.

Withdrawal of the Legion

On 27 April 1943, the surviving members of the Dutch Legion were withdrawn from the front line and transferred to the Grafenwöhr training area for a period of rest. With the Legion officially disbanded, Himmler convinced the Dutch volunteers to stay to fight alongside the German armed forces. After having seen with how much passion and courage the European volunteers had fought on the Eastern Front, both Himmler and SS-*Obergruppenführer* Gottlob Berger, head of the *SS-Hauptamt* (the SS Central Office), decided to transform the Legions into larger independent units, include them officially in the *Waffen SS*, and upgrade them to new brigades or divisions. Formation of the *SS-Panzergrenadier Nederland Brigade* was initiated using the Dutch volunteers.

Bibliography
Massimiliano Afiero, "23.*SS-Freiwilligen-Panzergrenadier-Division Nederland*", Associazione Culturale Ritterkreuz
Massimiliano Afiero, "*The 23rd Waffen SS Vol.Pz.Gr.Div. Nederland*", Schiffer Publishing
Charles Trang, "*Dictionnaire de la Waffen SS, volume 4*", Heimdal Editions

Zvonimir Bernwald
13. SS-Division 'Handschar' and 31. SS-Division
by Peter Mooney

SS-Uscha. **Zvonimir Bernwald.**

Soldiers of the *Leibstandarte*.

Zvonimir Bernwald was born in what we know today as Croatia, in August 1924. His father had served in the Austro-Hungarian Army during the First World War, but following that, was a Cooper (barrel maker). His family's position was modest and he grew up in a country that already contained many ethnic and religious 'challenges'. That region was Serbian dominated Yugoslavia. The invasion of that country in April 1941 and the rapid conclusion of the German campaign there, resulted in the creation of separate states. Croatia was pro-German and mainly muslim, with Serbia being anti-German and mostly communist. Zvonimir recalls seeing the *Leibstandarte SS-Adolf Hitler* near his home in 1941, as they moved there on their way from Greece. The then 16-year old Zvonimir began to earn some summer money, helping translate for the increasing number of Germans located where he lived. That was against the backdrop of increasing tensions coming to the fore, with Partisan activity and attacks beginning too.

In late-1942 he volunteered for the *Waffen-SS*, following a recruitment drive in Croatia. His first location was Lichterfelde in Berlin, being placed with the same *Leibstandarte SS-Adolf Hitler* he had seen 18-months earlier. One of his brothers served with the German Police in Italy, with the other finding his way to Tito's Partisans. His first two months were in Berlin, before he moved to France and began a short stint with SS-Division *'Das Reich'*. In this introductory phase to life within the *Waffen-SS*, he was taught on various weapons, up to the light anti-tank gun. The physical aspects of the training took their toll on many of his Croatian friends, who were dismissed. Zvonimir himself suffered a hernia and was sent to recover in the SS military hospital in Dachau. After his treatment, he was placed with the Motorcycle Replacement Battalion in Ellwangen. His next significant change came about, when a call was put out for anyone who could read and write the Serbo-Croat language. He had put himself forward, in response to the above call, and found himself back near Berlin, only this time in Oranienburg, at the SS-Interpreter School. Towards the end of April 1943, he was then sent to the SS-Main Office in Berlin. Zvonimir was put on the staff of the fledgling Croatian SS formation, which would become the *13. SS-Division 'Handschar'*. His role was to fill in the extensive gaps of knowledge that the SS possessed, when trying to consider the requirements for forming this unusual SS formation.

Volunteers begin the selection process to become members of *Handschar*.

Photo of Imams group taken in Babelsberg, Zvonimir is 4th from left, rear.

He became a central figure in devising answers to a long list of queries, as they worked through the 'rules and regulations' that would be necessary for the volunteers that would join this upcoming new formation. In the summer of 1943, he himself attended an Imams course, which contained the group that would be responsible for the spiritual guidance of the soldiers within *'Handschar'*. They pretty much began with a blank sheet of paper and between them, they drafted, discussed and finally completed the detailed training programme that each volunteer would need. That training programme focused on the spiritual, religious and world-politic views that were necessary, but not simple. The complication was trying to weld National Socialist and Islamic views into an agreed end result. One highlight for the course members, was the visit of the Grand Mufti of Jerusalem, who was the head of the Islamic faith in that area, but who was also considered a significant religious figure by all Muslims. Zvonimir was one of only two non-officers who was on this course. After the completion of that course, they all went to France, where the youthful Division was in the very early stages of their formation.

Handschar troops at morning prayer, whilst at Neuhammer in early 1944.

The *Handschar* officer and NCOs begin the search for the mutineers, whilst in France, 1943.

Zvonimir was placed with the Propaganda Platoon, who were responsible for printing the divisional magazine, aimed at providing the ideological material for the men to read. It was whilst in France that some volunteers from the Division, took part in a mutiny against the German officers. This was a contained mutiny and it was quickly crushed. However, the effects were wide ranging. Besides the death of 5 SS officers and the execution of the mutineers, hundreds of 'unfit' members of the division were removed and sent to concentration camps, where many of them subsequently died. Another key change, as a result of the mutiny, was the relocation of the remaining elements of the Division to Neuhammer, which is located in modern-day southwest Poland. They completed their training and formation at the training grounds there. The Grand Mufti visited the troops there, as did the *Reichsfuhrer-SS*, Heinrich Himmler. As 1944 opened, and against an increasingly worsening situation for the German military, the soldiers of the *13. SS-Division 'Handschar'*, the focus on the use of the weapons and tactics drew to a close.

The Grand Mufti during one of his visits in early 1944.

The difficulties of the fighting back in the former Yugoslavia were intensifying and the Communist Partisans, under Tito, were causing havoc. They were also mounting an effective propaganda campaign against the civilian population there.

Reichsfuhrer-SS, Heinrich Himmler, visits the *Handschar* troops.

Handschar recruits take their oath of allegiance - the differences in the placing of their hands is evident.

News of all of these unfolding situations were making their way to the men back in Neuhammer and they were unsettling them; they all wanted to get back to Croatia and Bosnia and play their part in defending their own homeland. They were to soon get their wish. Before the end of February 1944, the first elements of *Handschar* began their moves to Bosnia. They began taking part in military operations very soon after that. Starting in early March, they participated in series of operations throughout the next 6-months, which had varying results. They suffered some significant losses, but also managed to destroy or capture Partisans and partisan equipment. They were operating under many difficulties alongside the 'obvious' ones presented by their enemy.

Karl-Gustav Sauberzweig (second from the left) the commander of the *'Handschar'*.

Handschar troops during their deployment in Bosnia.

Operationally, their deployment was not considered as effective as it could have been. Also, new formations were raised, which weakened *Handschar*. By September, the above-mentioned worsening military situation for the Germans, resulted in increasingly large numbers of deserters from the ranks of *Handschar*, who were now in their homeland and were very concerned for the safety of their families. They all took their weapons and training with them and an unknown number of them changed sides and went over to Tito's forces. The decreasing confidence in the Germans, by the Bosnians, was also made worse by the German support of the Chetniks.

Handschar troops in a Bosnian village, 1944.

Handschar troops marching in Bosnia, 1944.

Artillerymen of the *Handschar* in action.

They were an alternative enemy for Tito and his men, but the Chetniks and the Muslims of *Handschar*, did not see eye to eye. The supply of weapons and other aid to the Chetniks was not welcomed by the men of *Handschar* and the 'faith' they had in the Germans as their 'saviour's was diminishing rapidly. Up to the end of June 1944, Zvonimir continued his role with the Propaganda unit of *Handschar* located in Bosnia. They were employed in the creation of further editions of the divisional magazine, as well as recruitment drives to obtain more volunteers, which was becoming increasingly difficult. He recalled that the people were more interested in food and clothes, rather than being shown a recruitment film. From July to October 1944, he was sent to Graz in Austria and took part in an officer's candidate course there. That was immediately followed by attendance at an officer's training course in Keinschlag, Czech Protectorate, where he graduated with the rank of *SS-Standartenoberjunker*. He returned to frontline service, only this time being placed with the 31. *Freiwilligen Grenadier Division der Waffen-SS*, serving in the role of Kompanie Commander. They were located near Warsaw. He saw out the remainder of the war there, being promoted to *SS-Untersturmführer* on the 20th of April 1945. Following the surrender, he began a difficult journey through southwest Poland, into Czecheslovakia, aiming to make his way to Germany.

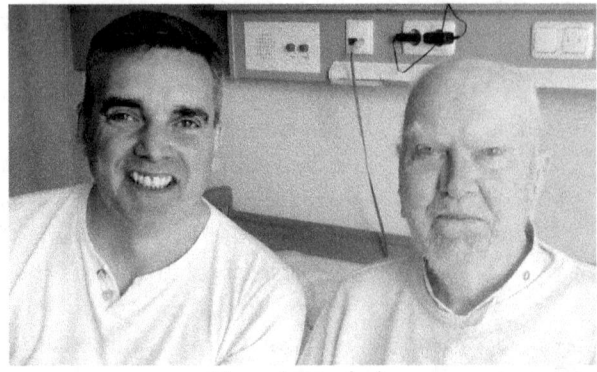

Me and Zvonimir.

He aimed to disguise himself as a displaced Yugoslavian worker. He had some luck and many 'adventures' during this stage of his story. His 'identity' was finally uncovered in Bavaria, where his stint as a former *Waffen-SS* prisoner of war began. What followed was just over 2 years on internment in various camps, until his eventual release in late-1947. Following this, Zvonimir began a difficult phase of his life, trying to find work and secure a future for himself and his family (which came along too). He had some luck along the way and by 1960, he began a successful career with a Swiss printing firm who instrumental in devising innovative printing techniques, which went worldwide. At the time of this article, Zvonimir Bernwald lives in southwest Bavaria. In 2012, Zvonimir Bernwald had his history of the *13. SS-Division 'Handschar'* printed in the German language. In late-2018, he was very pleased to see his book finally published in his native Bosnian language – something that would have been unheard of 20-years earlier.

"For the Defence of my nation – Bosnians in the Waffen-SS: The recollections of Zvonimir Bernwald"

My discussions and face to face contact with Herr Bernwald began in early 2018 (thanks to my friend, Jimmy Mcloed in Scotland). That has resulted in the translation and printing of the above titled book, by *Loyalty and Honour Publishing*. The book itself is expected to be available from the end of January 2019. Please go to www.lahpublishing.com for details of the book, pricing and how to obtain your own copy. There will be a limited number of signed bookplates available too. The above new book contains chapters on Zvonimir's childhood, service in the Waffen-SS, NCO and officer training and final stages of the conflict, as well as his challenging post-war experiences. It also has chapters devoted to the Imams of the *Waffen-SS*, the Grand Mufti of Jerusalem, the mutiny in France, the history of Bosnia-Herzegovina and finishes off with a chapter on his *'Handschar'* Kameraden's post-war experiences and various trials. This is a rare opportunity to read the recollections of someone who served in one of the *Waffen-SS'* foreign divisions, but one where the welding of National Socialist and Muslim ideologies was undertaken. His book was written to provide the facts of what took place, and to counter the many mis-representations that have been written about *'Handschar'* since the end of the war; his words are now available in English for the first time.

The Barbarigo Battalion on the Anzio front
By Massimiliano Afiero – 3rd part

Littoria, April 1944: the first copy of the battalion journal.

On April 1, 1944, the first copy of the battalion journal, entitled with the unit's name, arrived for the Marò of the Barbarigo, a single page printed in a hurry in an abandoned print shop in Littoria. On that same day, a report arrived from General von Mackensen, commander of the 14th Armee, on the behavior of the Barbarigo on the front line: "... *Barbarigo Battalion. The officers and non-commissioned officers have high morale, poor command experience in combat, they are happy being in the front line and volunteer for reconnaissance attacks and patrols The troops are young, with scant training and no combat experience. Under the constant supervision of German commanders so far they have behaved well in combat, in outposts.*

German soldiers and a *Panther* tank on the Anzio Front, Spring 1944.

Under artillery fire and bombing so far they have been irreproachable, but they have not been engaged in any major action. In general, they try hard to make up for their lack of experience, to match the performance of the German soldier. It is not sure if this battalion can withstand a serious attack (barrage fire or heavy bombardment) ". Naturally the report did not take into account the logistical difficulties that the Italian battalion had to face and overcome.

A 88mm *Flak* Battery on the Anzio Front, Spring 1944.

From left, a German officer, Bardelli and Borghese.

Nettuno: girls from Women's Auxiliary Service.

On 6 April 1944, a patrol led by Sergeant Giuseppe Trovatello, while on patrol in no-man's-land, in front of the *"Erna"* strongpoint, clashed with an American patrol. In the ensuing gunfight, an American soldier was killed and three prisoners were captured, immediately taken to the rear, while there were no losses on the Italian side.

A visit by the commander, Junio Valerio Borghese

Sunday, April 9, 1944, Easter Day, the battalion commander Borghese came to visit the battalion: after a quick meeting with the officers, he went to the front line, inspecting the positions of the 2nd and 4th companies. There were also gift packages, distributed, to the great surprise of the marines, by the girls of the not yet officially constituted Women's Auxiliary Service, the first women admitted into the Italian armed forces. There was also the customary official speech to the battalion by the commander: "... *You have been placed in the front line, welcomed with the most fraternal camaraderie by our*

German allies, who are also happy not to be alone in the heroic undertaking to make our will triumph over matter, with only minimal training. Some of you came from the Navy, some from civilian life, and a few of you had already experienced the water of the foxholes and the sound of exploding shells. Only a few days there were enough to give you experience, the experience, the skill of the veteran. It is the spirit that animates you, the beautiful spirit, combative, scornful and dashing of the volunteers of the Xa *and* S.Marco *that makes you the first soldiers of the Armed Forces of the new Italy. Marines of the* **Barbarigo**! *Comrades of yours have fallen as heroes in their combat positions, and others have already distinguished themselves by their perfect behaviour.*

Borghese with Capitano Carnevale, commander of The *San Giorgio* artillery group.

All of you are good soldiers. Other battalions of the San Marco *are in training and will come to relieve you, and then others and others, as long as an Englishman, an American or a Russian is still on Italian soil ...."*. Commander Borghese stayed two days with his marines, and then went to the headquarters of Field Marshal Albert Kesserling on Mount Soratte.

Back in the forefront

On 10 April 1944, the III Company returned to the front line, taking a position between the Strada Nascosta junction, Strada della Persicara and Lake Fogliano, taking over from IV Company, which in turn was transferred to Sezze. The III Company had to also man the strongpoints of *"Dora"*, *"Erna"* and *"Frida"* in no man's land. Of particular importance was strongpoint *"Dora"*, in the center, located about three kilometers beyond the main line of combat, in the direction of the Mussolini Canal. The outpost was completely surrounded by minefields and there were two paths to reach it, one that connected with the main lines and one for the patrols that led to enemy lines. For its defense, there were two teams, one Italian and one German, for a total of 25-26 men, under the orders of a German sergeant. The *Barbarigo* team was under the command of Sergeant Elio Ferrini. The other two outposts were located on the flanks, one on the left of a water-pumping plant and the other, the northernmost of the three, in a large rural farm near Cerreto.

A well-camouflaged 88mm Flak gun on the Anzio Front.

First Special Service Force patrol near Cerreto Alto.

Sherman tanks before an attack, Spring 1944.

German prisoners captured during the attack of the *First Special Service Force* on Cerreto Alto, April 1944.

On the other hand, the enemy was preparing to attack precisely in the sector between Cerreto Alto and the sea. The attack, scheduled for the night between April 14 and 15 and which was to be conducted by *First Special Service Force* patrols supported by tanks, had three main objectives: the Idrovora di Fogliano (for a diversionary attack), a group of houses at the intersection of the coastal road and the road to Fogliano and the large farm at Cerreto Alto. For the Axis forces those three places constituted the strongpoints "*Frida*", "*Erna*" and "*Dora*". Around midnight, a first enemy platoon moved towards the Fogliano Idrovora, for a diversionary action to cover the two main attacks. Around 3:00, they attacked two other enemy groups. At dawn the armored units also began to move, *Sherman* tanks of the 1st Armored Regiment, *Stuart* tanks and armored cars of the 81st Reconnaissance Battalion and a self-propelled platoon of the 701st Tank Destroyer Battalion. This armored mass passed the Mussolini Canal near Borgo Sabotino, continuing to advance to link up with the patrols of the *First Special Service Force*. As soon as the tanks arrived, around 5:30 am, the 4th Company of the FSSF moved forward along the coastal road and after having made it through a minefield, attacked the "*Erna*" strongpoint. The *Shermans* in support immediately opened fire against the Italian and German positions, which were well camouflaged in a group of ruined houses. While some *Shermans* continued to fire at the strongpoint, keeping out of range of the *Panzerfausts*, another group of tanks, advancing in single file, broke into the strongpoint. The Italian and German artillery held their fire so as not to kill their own comrades. At about 9:00 am, the FSSF's 4th Company returned to its positions, after killing six of the Axis defenders and capturing 42 prisoners, without suffering losses. Meanwhile the 5th Company of the FSSF, after arriving in the locality of "Le Vergini", took the road to Cerreto, to attack the *"Dora"* strongpoint. After making it through a minefield, the Allied troops got to within a hundred meters of the position. There, they waited until dawn and the arrival of supporting tanks to begin the attack.

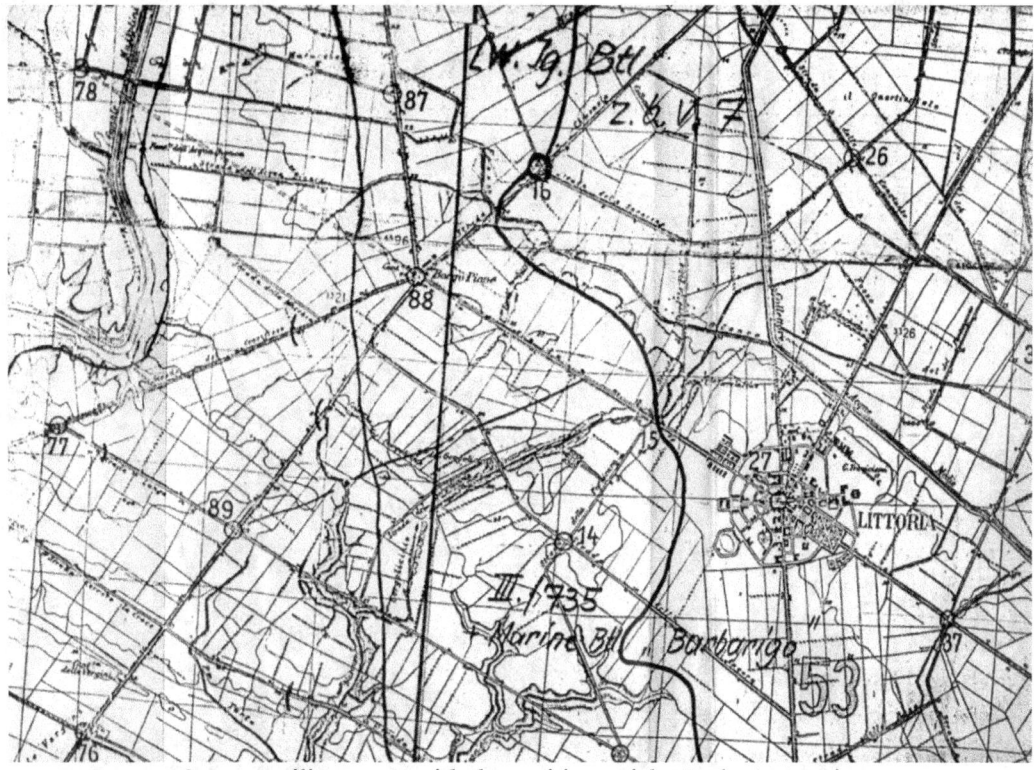

German military map with the positions of the *Barbarigo*'s units.

A *Sherman* tank on the Anzio Front.

At about 7:00 am, two *Stuart* tanks arrived at the intersection about two kilometers from the town. The Italian and German defenders opened fire on the enemy. The enemy tanks in turn began to fire on the strongpoint, while the infantry began to advance towards it. When all seemed lost, the Italian and German artillery began to hit the whole area around the outpost, especially the 65mm guns of the *Barbarigo's* 5th Cannon Company. Overwhelmed by this deluge of fire, the enemy tanks retreated, under the cover of a smokescreen, leaving two tanks knocked out. The Allied infantry also fell back, taking nineteen prisoners with them. The diversionary attack against the Idrovora di Fogliano consisted mainly of interdiction fire by machine guns and mortars, which only caused the evacuation of a small Italo-German strongpoint. At the end of the attack, the Allied units took 61 prisoners, 17 of them Italians.

April 1944: defensive position of the II Company of *Barbarigo*.

A marine of the *Barbarigo* engaged in combat.

According to Allied sources, there were 19 Italian and German casualties. After this umpteenth enemy attack, it was decided to transform the system of fixed strongpoints in the no man's land into mobile strongpoints linked by patrols. In particular, the III Company of *Barbarigo*, kept four men at the "*Frida*" strongpoint and a patrol of three men along the shore of Lago di Fogliano.

The artillery of the Decima blocks the enemy tanks

Let us listen to the testimony of Lieutenant Giulio Cencetti, about these latest actions[1]: "... *The dawn of April 15 '44. Phosphorous and smoke shells hit the area of the 'second'. This time it isn't the usual artillery fire. The unmistakable 'go and come' of the self-propelled guns hit the positions, mercilessly and furiously. The second platoon is invested and the fire spreads to the right on the holes of the 'third' and 'first'. If these two positions are attacked simultaneously, what can Monticelli do? It is clear that this is not an attack that will peter out quickly. Sergeant Mazio takes command of the company, with a note from Ensign Falangola:* 'There are a lot of them and they are getting close. Strongpoint Erna has fallen and been bypassed...*

A gun of the *San Giorgio* artillery group on the Anzio Front, Spring 1944.

A 105 mm Self Propelled Gun, *Priest*.

The Americans attacking strongpoint 'Dora'. The Germans are pulling out, so I had to put two of our men on the 47mm gun'. *The company command post has been surrounded... The shouts of the Tommies are heard in the fog. The lieutenant sends marò Poli to the 3rd Platoon:* 'Let Lieutenant Posio with his weapons, as far as he is able, make his way to the lines of the 2nd Platoon'. 'OK', *says Polacci as he returns, who seems to have found the way between one burst and the other ...* 'Polacci!', 'Comandi!', 'Go as fast as you can and tell Lieutenant Monticelli *that the Gorgolicino is a deep enough ditch, and when they get there have them take cover in it'. But how what are we going to do against the tanks with our 47mm guns? Sergeant Malagnini is killed instantly. Strongpoint 'Dora' falls under the attacks, overwhelmed along with all of its defenders. 'Polacci!', 'Yes, sir', he answers with panting breath. 'Run to Lieutenant Trettene of the 5th Cannon Company, bring him this'. 'I'm from the 5th Cannon and it's Lieutenant Trettene who sends me to put at your disposal', says a sergeant, who has come crawling. Well, then write quickly:* 'Lieutenant Trettene, strongpoints Erna and Dora have fallen. Enemy infantry supported by tanks advancing trying to overwhelm II / 2 positions, threatening III / 2. Fire all of your rounds on Cerreto Alto is effective. Please follow the movement of tanks by direct observation and act accordingly ... '.

Allied tanks destroyed in front of *Barbarigo* positions, Spring 1944.

The waiting minutes drag onto centuries. The tanks are now two hundred meters from the positions. The fire of the German artillery and our '105' goes too far, it is long. When you are on the ground, there is always confusion with the medium calibres, and it is goodbye difference between 'interdiction' and 'barrier'. Finally, it is an old and dear voice that is 'heard': that of 65/17, familiar to Lieutenant Trettene of the 5th Cannon and to the lieutenant commanding the 2nd Company, which furrows the air. The rounds pass over the heads of the marines hit a tank, which is close to another one, and hit the tracks of a third. Pardella quietly urges his gunners on, because the faster the fire, the geater the chances of success. Trettene sees the tanks stop. Between falling shells, one backs up and the other also turns away. He orders changes in range: shorter, longer, change direction, increase range again. Trettene sends wordy, almost shouts, to the commander of the Second, who now has only twenty rounds left. 'Everyone get out of here, Memmo. Let's go, boys'. *And Erna and Dora were retaken*".

New attacks

In the days that followed, the fighting continued with greater intensity, once again involving the II Company sector, which was attacked in force by units of the *First Special Service force*. The enemy was trying to break through the front using all means at his disposal. On 19 April, the positions of the 2nd Platoon were attacked along the Strada Nascosta, being first subjected to heavy enemy artillery shelling. Sergeant De Angelis gathered his men around him, ordering them to take cover from the enemy fire. But it was all in vain, because the hurricane of fire unleashed by the enemy took many victims: marines Brembati, Draghi, Carrozzo, Scudellari and message runner Alfeo Polacci all fell. All of the other men were wounded, among them De Angelis himself, with a mangled leg. When the attack ended, there were eight dead and six wounded. In order to avoid any new enemy incursions, the order was given to reinforce all of the Italian defensive positions. On 22 April, the IV Company was shifted along the Malconsiglio road, behind the rear area of the front; its training continued to be carried out there and at the same time, its men were engaged in fortification works in the area of Coppola and the woods in front of it. On 24 April, during a new incursion by a patrol of enemy special units in the Cerreto Alto area two marines were captured, despite the massive barrier fire unleashed by Italian machine guns. The next day, enemy artillery fire continued to claim victims within II Company; one shell scored a direct hit on the command post, killing seven marines and wounding another six. Then, when other marines approached the building to give aid to their comrades, enemy artillery continued to fire, causing yet more victims. It was a real massacre, due mainly to the marines' lack of front-line experience. During the night between 26 and 27 April, mixed patrol activity was resumed, formed by marines of the IV Company and by German grenadiers, engaged in actions in no-man's-land. On 1 May, marines of II Company were engaged in patrol activity, with the mission of destroying several houses used as strongpoints by the enemy. On 27 April, capitano di corvetta (lieutenant commander) Umberto Bardelli relinquished command of the *Barbarigo* to assume command of the 1st Naval Infantry Regiment of the new Decima Division then being formed[2]. His place was taken by capitano di corvetta Giuseppe Vallauri. At the end of April, a new enemy attack was launched against the sector of the front defended by IV Company, which at that time was deployed along the Gorgolicinio ditch. The enemy soldiers ended up in the barbed wire entanglements, on which empty tin cans had been hung to give the alarm. A massive barrage fire erupted from the Italian foxholes, forcing the Americans to withdraw.

Notes

[1] From "*Gli ultimi in grigioverde*", pag. 1091, 1092.

[2] At that time, thanks to the influx of new volunteers, the formation of the Decima Naval Infantry Division was begun. Its structure included two infantry regiments, one of artillery and a pioneer battalion. The *Barbarigo*, NP and *Lupo* battalions formed the 1st Regiment. The Alpine Sapper battalions *Valanga*, *Sagittario* and *Fulmine* formed the 2nd Regiment.

Bibliography
Mario Bordogna, "*Junio Valerio Borghese e la X^a Flottiglia MAS*", Mursia, Milano, 2007
Guido Bonvicini, "*Decima Marinai! Decima Comandante!*", Mursia, Milano
Daniele Lembo, "*I fantasmi di Nettunia*", Edizioni Settimo Sigillo
Marino Perissinotto, "*Duri a morire - storia del Battaglione Barbarigo*", Ermanno Albertelli
Perissinotto, Panzarasa, "*Come la Fenice*", Editoriale Lupo
Giorgio Pisanò, "*Gli ultimi in grigioverde*", C.D.L. Edizioni

The Axis Forces

THE PRICE OF THE OATH
The last battle of the Charlemagne Division
by Tomasz Borowski

Oberstleutnant **Krukenberg.**

On the night of 23/24 April, *SS-Brigadeführer* Krukenberg was called to Berlin to take command of a new unit. Much has been written of that night, but where is the truth? According to Gustav Krukenberg's own recollections[1], he had received two calls around 4:00 a.m. on 24 April. The first call was from *Personalamt der Waffen-SS* (The Personnel Office of the *Waffen-SS*) in Furstenberg, the other from Army Group Vistula command in Prenzlau. Both calls relayed the orders from OKW[2] to immediately report to Berlin to take command of a division whose former CO had become ill. After his arrival, Krukenberg was to report to the Reich Chancellery to General Hans Krebs (the Army Chief-of-Staff) and *SS-Obergruppenführer* Hermann Fegelein, communications officer for the *Waffen-SS* and Adolf Hitler's HQ. Krukenberg asked about the situation in Berlin. He was informed that the Soviets had broken the lines along the Oder and commenced their final offensive to conquer Berlin. It was just a matter of hours before the capital was completely surrounded. The *LVI.Panzer-Korps* stationed on the east side of the city was pushed back to the suburbs and engaged in heavy defensive fighting[3]. In spite of the hopeless situation, Krukenberg was told that *"our commander"* made contact with *"the leader of our enemies in the West"*.

March, 1945. One of the very last photos of Adolf Hitler. On the right, Hermann Fegelein.

German soldiers engaged in fighting on the outskirts of Berlin, 1945.

The Americans had already arrived at the River Elbe and the defence in the region was to be put on hold to allow them to get to Berlin before the Red Army or – in the worst case scenario – right along with it[4]. Beyond that, the *XXXI.Panzer-Korps*[5], under the command of General Wenck (commander of the Twelfth Army), stationed near Rathenow-Genthin, had received orders to move their forces towards Potsdam. This was meant to open up a corridor for the Americans to move towards the western outskirts of Berlin and allow them to take the city districts there. Krukenberg took a moment to think. He asked himself: how do you defend a city that still has several million inhabitants?[6] In June 1940, Paris was declared an open city, sparing its people the horror of street warfare.

Soviet tanks move into Prussia, 1945.

General Walter Wenck.

East Prussian refugees, 1945.

The soldiers of the Red Army, however, had been known to rape, plunder and steal everything in their path through West Prussia and Pomerania. If Berlin was to fall into their hands, the same fate awaited those who lived there. The capital had been declared a stronghold on 1 February, since when work on her defences has been in full force, so maybe the city was defensible? Given the uncertainty of the situation and the fear of what may be waiting for him in Berlin, Krukenberg asked permission to take with him a few of his comrades and a special escort. The Army Group Vistula Staff agreed and also informed him that the way to Berlin through Oranienburg and Frohnau was still clear of enemy troops and was the best path to the capital. As evidenced in the memoirs of Robert Soulat[7], at 3:00 a.m., *SS-Brigadeführer* Gustav Krukenberg received a cable ordering him to use the remnants of *'Charlemagne'* Division to form an assault battalion, and to take them the quickest way to Berlin and report to the Reich Chancellery[8]. There are many differing accounts of whether or not Krukenberg had indeed received a cable calling the *'Charlemagne'* Division to Berlin, and whether or not his escort was to be in full battalion strength or just 90 men? *SS-Obersturmführer* Weber had seen the cable as well[9].

Soviet artillery at the Seelow Heights, April 1945.

SS-Ostuf. Otto Günsche.

Henri Fenet in civilian clothes.

It was sent from Adolf Hitler's own HQ (*Führerhauptquartier*) and bore his own signature. After the war, this account was confirmed by *SS-Sturmbannführer* Otto Günsche[10], Hitler's aide, who claimed to have sent that exact cable personally. According to many French and German veterans of all ranks, the socalled escort accompanying Krukenberg to Berlin had indeed the strength of a battalion[11]. Beyond that, in order to settle this debate, it is worth reaching for the report made by Pz.AOK 3 (Third Panzer Army) on 24 April, which states that the command staff and the "*1.Batl.33 SS-WGD. Charlemagne*" marched on Berlin. The name *'Charlemagne'* never appears in the official documents again, but is mentioned as Assault Group 'Fenet' (*Kampfgruppe Fenet*) from the name of its commanding officer, or as the French SS Assault Battalion (*Franzosische SS-Sturmbataillon*)[12]. Having received phone calls and cables, *SS-Brigadeführer* Krukenberg called a briefing of all his officers in his HQ in the castle of Carpin, where he informed them of the decisions. *SS-Hauptsturmführer* Henri Fenet arrived first. He was greeted by a smiling Krukenberg and told of the circumstances surrounding Berlin[13].

Heavily equipped German Panzergrenadiers in undergrowth during defensives actions in 1945.

German soldiers armed with *Panzerfaust*, 1945.

Waffen-SS soldier with a *MG-42* in combat, 1945.

Fenet was very satisfied with what he heard. Officers had arrived one by one and gathered in the hallway, speaking in hushed voices, when the door suddenly opened and Krukenberg joined them. Without any preamble, he told them the Russians would soon reach Berlin. He told them he was being called to the capital to take command of a new formation and that they could join him and defend Berlin to the very end. He proposed to enter the city from the north through the town of Oranienburg. The French *Waffen-SS* officers listened to Krukenberg speak, open-mouthed and in complete silence. Finally, it dawned on them what they were in for: Berlin, the Chancellery, the last battle. The capital seemed to them a symbolic blaze of glory, ever surrounded in myth. *Führer* Hitler had made his choice: to either see victory there or his death, and the Russians were ready to take the city as quickly as possible[14]. The news of the Berlin mission spread like wildfire. Every soldier had a decision to make: fight until the end or stay behind?[15] The unit was formed immediately. It was formed of the entirety of the *57.SS-Bataillon*[16], one company from the *58.SS-Bataillon*[17] and the Honour Guard (*Kampfschule*). Rostaing and his men were filled with pride, as they were the only company from the *58.Bataillon* chosen for the march to Berlin. All other assault units from '*Charlemagne*' were prepared to march in the second echelon, the day after[18].

The Axis Forces

A German soldier takes aim with a *Sturmgewehr 44* assault rifle during the last months of World War II.

Troops take cover in a trench during a lull in the battle.

Waffen-SS soldiers in front of an *Sd.Kfz.251*, 1945.

Weapons and ammunition were distributed. Almost every grenadier from the *57.Bataillon* was armed with an automatic *Sturmgewehr 44* assault gun. Rostaing's company's volunteers were not so lucky: only one in every three soldiers received the weapon. Each platoon was equipped with a heavy machine gun MG 42 (*Maschinengewehr 42*). They did not forget about the mighty RPGs – the panzerfausts. For the first and last time, they received generous food rations, though many soldiers preferred to stow ammunition in their pockets rather than food. Earlier, around 10 April, the unit had received new camouflage uniforms, including jackets and camouflage trousers made from eau-de-nil pattern dungarees, Erbstarnmuster. Once again, Rostaing's men came up short as there weren't enough sets for them. They only got the pants, whilst the upper body uniform was replaced with normal sweatshirts made of *feldgrau* material. Robert Soulat states that he and his comrades were never in as good a shape as they were at that moment. Indeed, their enthusiasm reminded him of *"all those victorious German soldiers from the first days of the war"*. Their morale was superb, and for the first time, what he saw in their eyes was a strange flame. They were positively yearning for the upcoming fight for life or death, as if they already knew what was in store for them[19]. After the war, Louis Levast, a soldier from the 'Charlemagne' Division's *Kampfschule*, spoke in similar tones, if with a little more fatalism: *"...In mid-April, General Krukenberg told us we had the honour of participating in the defence of Berlin, along with other* Charlemagne *companies, all 700 of us. To be exact, he said:*

'Comrades, we are chosen by [the] Führer himself to stand at his side and defend the Reich's capital against the European invasion, led by the Soviet hordes. By our fight and sacrifice we shall not let the Red savages enter. Sieg Heil'. *Everyone took this speech with enthusiasm, with screams of 'Hurray!', already picturing themselves standing hand-in-hand with Adolf Hitler. We did not have any illusions, however: we didn't believe in new weapons any more. All we had left was to fight until the end to honour our vows and to go down fighting rather than somewhere in a ditch, with a bullet in our backs. The decision to march on Berlin was a true relief. As for me, I told myself in petto*[20]*, as our group was busy building anti-tank trenches: 'They'll shoot me in a ditch just as this one'.*"[21]

A German defensive position with a *MG-42*.

Heinrich Himmler.

The French Assault Battalion left Carpin at 5:30 a.m. on 24 April and headed for Alt-Sterlitz. From there, at 8:30 a.m., they moved towards Berlin in a convoy of a couple of regular cars and some 15 Ford V 3005 trucks borrowed from the *Luftwaffe*, each vehicle packed beyond capacity, carrying around 40 men[22]. While the French SS-men prepared for departure to Alt-Sterlitz, they saw a black Mercedes limousine heading for them at top speed. Behind the wheel was none other than *Reichsführer-SS* Himmler. Krukenberg, his aide Pachur and the duty officer, Patzak, stood to attention at once. The *Mercedes* passed by the column at a slower pace, but it did not stop. Himmler did not even look at them. The car disappeared in the distance as quickly as it appeared. All three were surprised and obviously disappointed: the *Reichsführer-SS* did not stop to inspect their troops.

After a moment's reflection, they all went about their business. After the war, Krukenberg spoke of this incident: "*Later on, I discovered Himmler must have been on his way back from meeting Count Bernadotte in Lubeck. He was sure to know of our orders. If he wanted to negotiate a cease-fire, he should've stopped us from going to Berlin or, at the very least, made us aware of the situation. I have no doubt that by passing us by, he simply wanted to avoid this painful necessity*"(23).

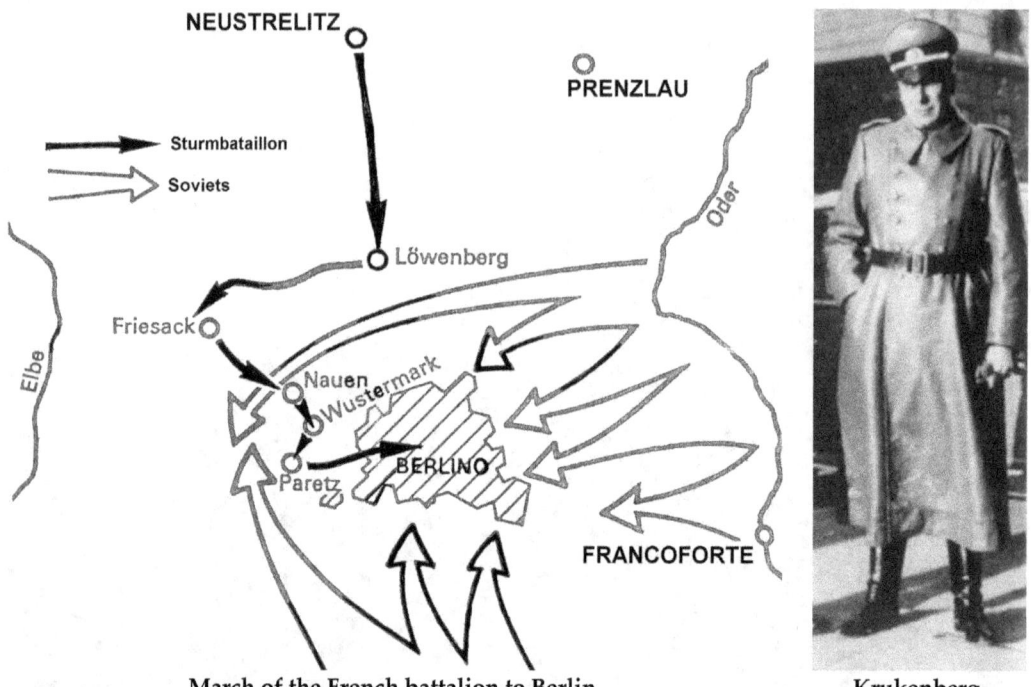

March of the French battalion to Berlin.   Krukenberg.

Waffen-SS soldiers, 1945.

Their preparations complete, the convoy embarked towards Berlin between 8:30 and 9:00 am. It was comprised of 400-500(24) volunteers and headed south. They had about 100 km to cover. Pierre Rostaing remembers this time: "*At 9, as it was planned, we all climbed up on the trucks, parked in a row on the huge Neustrelitz square. Soon the convoy moved and drove at break-neck pace towards the agonized Reich's capital. We sang: "Forward, close the ranks, This is our song, Our war song, the song of victory That brings hope." We forgot our language, speaking only in German. What matters it now, though? We stopped being Germans – or Frenchmen. We were only but a beachhead of some dying Europe*"(25).

Road to fate

The convoy was moving south, passing refugees heading in the opposite direction. Traffic jams formed. The Frenchmen also passed by former prisoners of concentration camps in Oranienburg and Ravensbruck. Civilians and soldiers alike were surprised to see a transport moving, seemingly, straight into the lion's mouth. In every town, they had to push through gridlocks and traffic jams caused by escaping refugees and retreating soldiers. When passing through Nauen, the French column came under fire from the Soviet air force, but managed to escape unharmed. When they made the turn towards Wustermark, they saw their path was under enemy fire. Krukenberg remembered there was another road, through Ketzin towards Marquart, which was supposed to be available. The convoy turned in that direction at around noon on 24 April.

Waffen-SS **soldiers waiting to mount on trucks.**

Waffen-SS **soldier with a** *MG-42.*

A group of German soldiers, Spring 1945.

After having covered some 6 Km without incident, they saw a Soviet unit in the distance. Luckily, it was small and lacking heavy weaponry. This was one of the patrols from the Soviet spearhead surrounding Berlin: if they were to connect, Berlin would become cut off. The Russian troops also spotted the convoy and, wishing to avoid confrontation, started to retreat. Krukenberg mulled over his next step. What was he to do now? Should he turn back? There was absolutely nothing to ponder as there was no other option: orders were orders. The Russians had yet to take over the road they were on, so maybe they could make it, and this was their last chance to reach Berlin. But if they were to continue on their way, they might have to face the enemy and cross the stream around Falkenrehde farm. They did not know if the bridge over the channel was still standing? If they were to reach the stream and find no bridge, they would be unable to get to Berlin or turn back, as the Russians must have been nearby.

The Axis Forces

A column of vehicles carrying German troops, Spring 1945.

German soldiers during a withdrawal.

There were so many doubts for Krukenberg, but finally they moved forward, as quietly as possible. From that moment on, however, the column kept meeting obstacles, the Frenchmen feeling their good fortune had abandoned them. *SS-Oberjunker* Ginot's truck from Rostaing's company, closing up the convoy's rear, broke down. Luckily, Ginot was able to find a tow line and hook it up to the next working vehicle. Further ahead, near Brandenburg, two more trucks broke down and had to turn back. They were carrying some 90 men, including *Waffen-Obersturmführer* Fatin, as well as a medic, *Waffen-Obersturmführer* Dr. Herpe, and the chaplain, *Waffen-Untersturmführer* Verney. The remaining convoy had some 300-330 men left, hardly more than the Spartans had at Thermopylae[26]. Around 3:00 p.m., the Assault Battalion finally reached the bridge in Falkenrehde. It was still intact! If all went well, they would be in Berlin within an hour. First, though, they had to deal with a feeble anti-tank obstacle built across the road. The men were just about to get to work, when the bridge exploded right before their eyes. The force of the blast flung several of the nearest soldiers to the ground. A few ended up in the water. Thankfully, none of them were killed. One of the grenadiers was severely injured in the legs, several more – including Krukenberg – receiving light wounds. Aside from that, the explosion took his limousine out of commission. The 18-year-old *Waffen-Unterscharführer* Roberto, one of 'Fenet's gang', fell into the stream but managed to swim ashore. Two of his friends pulled him out. Despite having been partially blinded and stunned, Roberto refused to be sent to the rear[27]. Although the heavily damaged bridge was no longer viable for vehicles, they could still pass it on foot. Krukenberg quickly came back to his senses after the blast and gave orders to unload the trucks of all gear and equipment. The cars and the one poor badly wounded soldier were sent back to Neustrelitz, where they arrived without further trouble, despite having to drive through Soviet vanguards for several hours. Meanwhile, the grenadiers attempted to pass the broken bridge. On the other side, there were three old men from the *Volkssturm* (the German Home Guard, levée en masse) who admitted to having blown up the bridge. They were to do so as soon as they saw the enemy; they had mistaken the *Waffen-SS* convoy for the Russians. They now still had 20km to go to reach Berlin. They reformed the column and, burdened by their weapons and equipment, the Frenchmen set out to march at a quick pace. At the front, there was Krukenberg, limping and leaning on a stick, Fenet right at his side. Then there was Millet and Bicou, with Roberto in tow. Behind them marched Weber and his *Kampfschule*, then Michel's, Rostaing's and Ollivier's companies. The procession was completed by Labourdette, chivvying the stragglers along.

Waffen-Oscha. **Jean Ollivier** was the commanding officer of the 4th company.

They went west, kilometre after kilometre, ammunition and weapons getting heavier by the hour. They became soaked with sweat and white with dust, but to lift up their spirits, they sang. They crossed paths with more civilians and soldiers, heading in the opposite direction, the spectre of defeat painted on their faces. It turned out there was a group of some 40 former French POWs among them. They greeted their countrymen with applause, wishing them luck. Some of them even gave the SSmen some chocolate and American chewing gum. As night fell, Berlin was still well away. They passed by Gross Glienicke, Gatow and Pichelsdorf. Along their way, they saw nothing to indicate the defence of the capital was organized in any way. They only saw a handful of boys from the *Hitlerjugend* (Hitler Youth), armed with *panzerfausts* and riding bikes[28]. Eventually, they reached the bridge in Freybrucke across the River Havel, where they found a roadblock. The bridge itself wasn't guarded. Passing by Potsdam, having gone a much longer way, the companies finally reached Berlin from the south-west.5 Finally, around 10:00 p.m., the battalion arrived near the Olympic Stadium (*Reichssportfeld*) after a long and exhausting march of over 20km, in full gear, under the pressure of both enemy and time.....

Note

(1) Krukenberg wrote down his memoirs in 1964 and titled them Battle of Berlin. They have since been published by Robert Soulat, in Jean Mabire's book. Richard Landwehr edited them and published them as a chapter of his book under the title *Fighting for Berlin: A Battle Memoir*.

(2) *Oberkommando der Wehrmacht* (Supreme Command of the Armed Forces).

(3) Forbes, Robert, op.cit.

(4) Among the highest echelons of the Third Reich's leadership, it was widely believed that there was a possibility of division between the Western and Eastern allies and and – as a result – the chance for creating a joint front against the Soviet Union with the British and the Americans. Unofficial negotiation attempts had been made, but each and every time the Allies made the demand for the unconditional surrender of Nazi Germany.

(5) It was an armoured corps in name only. Their actual forces were severely weakened.

(6) Before the war, Berlin had 4.5 million inhabitants. It is difficult to estimate how many of them there were in April 1945. Many had fled from carpet bombings, but the city also received many refugees from the East, fleeing the marching Red Army.

(7) Soulat, op.cit., p.100.

(8) Soulat had seen the cable with his own eyes. He remembered it clearly as he had found it quite unusual.

(9) Both Mabire and Saint-Loup mention this. It is interesting to note, however, that both men recount the cable's content in different words.

This article is an extract from the book *"The price of the oath: the French ss Sturmbataillon during the battle of Berlin 1945"*, by Tomasz Borowski. The book is available directly from the author in e-book format. Price for complete book (250 pages main book + plus two colour sections and big Berlin map) is 7 GBP / 8 EUR. Paypal accepted. For more info: tobor2@wp.pl.

[10] After the war, Günsche was sentenced to imprisonment in Budziszyn, from where he was released in 1956. He died from heart disease at his home in Lohmar in 2003, leaving behind his three children.

[11] For example, Jean-Louis Puechlong, from *SS-Untersturmführer* Labourdette's company, in a letter from 24 November 1997 addressed to Robert Forbes, makes a note that his company had 85-90 men, including officers and NCOs, when they set out for Berlin.

[12] Forbes, Robert, op.cit.

[13] Mabire, Jean, *Berlin in Todeskampf 1945* (Nebel Verlag), p.110.

[14] Lefèvre, Eric, op.cit., p.16.

[15] According to Saint-Loup (p.382), during the briefing, Krukenberg ordered Fenet to gather company commanders Labourdette, Michel, Olliver, Rostaing and Weber, and to have them, in turn, explain to their men what was waiting for them and the two choices before them: to march for Berlin or stay at the rear. Krukenberg's order was followed, though every officer did so in their own way. Weber simply called his men to assembly and told them: *"Boys, we're going to defend Berlin. I hope none of the 6th company will break rank. Volunteers, to the front!"* Without hesitation, 125 men took a step forward as one man. One should make note that one of the officers from Rostaing's company (probably Ginot) claimed that Krukenberg came before all the Frenchmen gathered on the square and said: *"This is the moment. The Führer calls the French troops to him."* He continued to say he only wanted *"volunteers for the mission"* and if there were any, they should step forward. All of them did.

[16] Saint-Loup, op.cit., p.381.

[17] According to Soulat's letter to Robert Forbes, upon their leaving of Carpin, the *57.SS-Bataillon* had four companies, with *SS-Ostuf.* Fatin taking command of the 3rd one.

[18] It seems they didn't have enough transport capabilities to move the French volunteers all at once. In his book *Berlin in Todeskampf 1945,* Jean Mabire states that the first group was comprised of three companies from the *57.Bataillon*, the Staff and Weber's *Kampfschule*. They still had room for about 100 more men, so the command decided to add one more company from the *58.Bataillon*. They chose Rostaing's 6th Company as it was deemed most solid and best prepared for battle. The planned second echelon never left for Berlin, as all access routes soon became impassable.

[19] Forbes, Robert, op.cit.

[20] In a whisper.

[21] Levast, Louis, *Le soleil se couchait à l'est* (Editions de l'Homme Libre, 2008), p.99.

[22] Lefèvre, Eric, op.cit., p.17.

[23] It is widely known that Heinrich Himmler, through Count Folke Bernadotte – a representative of the Swedish Red Cross – was attempting negotiations with the Western Allies. Those attempts failed. Hitler learned of this betrayal on 28 April, and it was a huge blow to him. Betrayed by *"the most faithful of the faithful"*, he issued an arrest warrant for the former *Reichsführer-SS*. On the same day, he named Karl Hanke as the new *Reichsführer-SS*. You can find more on this subject in Peter Logerich's monumental biography of Himmler.

[24] Various authors provide varying accounts as to the number of volunteers that marched on the capital. Georgen believes there were 410-20 of them, Mabire and Landwehr 350, Sabine Roch 400 and Robert Soulat 500. Today it is impossible to ascertain the actual headcount of the formation.

[25] Rostaing, Pierre, *Le Prix d'un serment* (Editions du Paillon, 2008), p.160.

[26] Lefèvre, Eric, op.cit., p.17.

[27] Forbes, Robert, op.cit.

[28] Forbes, Robert, op.cit.

SS-Hauptsturmfuhrer Hans-Jörg Hartmann III Batl. 'Nordland' regiment 5th SS division "Wiking

By Ken Niewiarowicz – fourth and last part

This is a photo-essay based on a stack of Photo albums and documents from the estate of *SS-Hstuf.* Hans-Jörg Hartmann, born in Berlin-Licterfeld on October 21, 1913. The associated text is drawn from the captions of the photos as well as information in the documents that are associated with this grouping. The following photographs are in chronological order as they appear in the 2 wartime photo albums, compiled from photographs Hartmann between June and November 1941, while commanding 12th company in the campaign in the Ukraine.

Then onwards again....

Russian 'Elite' troops taken in front of Dniepropetrovsk.

Western Suburbs of Dniepropetrovsk.

The main train station on the western bank of the great Dnieper river.

Moving through Dniepropetrovsk.

Earlier, other units of *'Wiking'* had gotten across the 1600 meters of the Dneiper. Here, men are carrying ration containers into the bridgehead via a pontoon footbridge.

A heavier bridge was built to accommodate vehicle traffic.

Vehicles of *SS-Division 'Wiking'* in the Dniepropetrovsk bridgehead.

Knightscross holder *SS Gruppenführer und Generalleutnant der Waffen SS* Felix Steiner (indicated by the arrow in the photo), Commander of the *SS-Div. 'Wiking'*.

SS-Sturmbannführer Plöw, Commander III Battalion SS *'Nordland'*.

L'*SS-Sturmbannfuhrer* Plöw.

SS-Hstuf. Hartmann, commander 12. company.

Gli *SS-Ostuf.* Schröter and Müller (11. and 9. Company commanders). Schröter and some of his men would be killed in an action later on October 2.

The photo is captioned *'Breakthrough near Kamenka'*. The vehicle marking at right indicates a command vehicle of a Motorcycle mounted infantry platoon.

SS-Hstuf. Hartmann.

The Stalino Dam was blown up...

Safety in October 1941.

North of Mariupol - near the sea of Azov.

SS-Ostuf. Müller.   *SS-Ostuf.* Schröter has fallen along with 3 of his men.

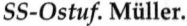

The death notice written by his wife:

"In the highest military tradition in the struggle against Bolschevism, my dear good-hearted husband; Hans-Jörg Hartmann Has fallen on November 20, 1941

Recipient of the Iron cross 1st and 2nd class, the wound badge and various other awards.

He gave his life for Germany.

Dorle Hartmann (Born Hembes) and children Werner and Hans-Jörg.

Klagenfurt, January 1942

SS Officer living quarters"

Romanian Armored Forces in World War II
Author: Eduardo M. Gil Martínez
Translator: Ricardo Ramallo Gil

A parade of Romanian Troops with *R-35* tanks.

Romanian FT-17 light tank on the Eastern front.

A *Škoda LT VZ 35* (R-2) tank on the Eastern front.

In this brief text we will try to remember the few known the Romanian armored forces during World War II (WWII). It's well known about the performance of the German armored forces during the war but what has not yet been so widespread is the behavior of the armored forces of Germany's allied countries. While it is true that the performance of these was usually quite secondary when not disappointing, we should highlight the behavior of the Romanian armored forces that in spite of the difficult situation, the played an important role in the Southern sector of the Eastern Front.

Romania realize the importance of the armored forces

On August 23, 1939 a secret pact of non-aggression was signed between the USSR and Germany (Ribbentrop-Molotov pact) in which both nations shared influences in Eastern Europe. On September 1 in the same year the German attack against Poland took place, which was the beginning of WWII. The beginning of the WWII with the German *Blitzkrieg* showed how important the armored forces would be in the newly initiated conflict. The Romanian government took note of this and as a first step a "Tank Training Center" was created in the vicinity of Târgoviste, where special emphasis could be placed on the new armored techniques that the Germans had in use. After that, it was neccesary to restructure its armored forces, which would be grouped at the end of 1939 in a large Brigade that was called 1st Motorized Brigade (*Brigade 1 motomecanizata* in Romanian), which included the 1st Tank Regiment equipped with 126 R-2 (Škoda LT VZ 35) and the 2nd Tank Regiment (created on November 1, 1939) with 75 R-35 (including both those purchased from France as well as the "gifts" from Poland). On the other hand, the venerable FT 17 were assigned to a training unit called the FT tank battalion (*Batalionul Carelor de Lupta FT*), reaching a theoretical number of 75 but the real number of FT tank in service was about 20-30, which would fulfill the functions of inner security in the country (in 1944 these armored relics still fulfilled surveillance tasks in the Romanian capital).

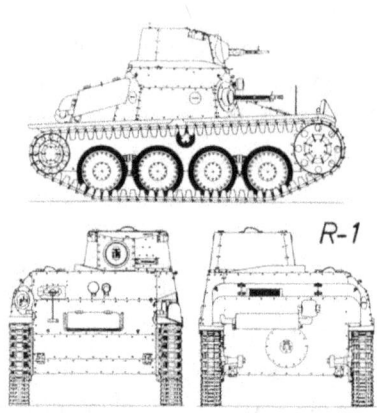

Technical profile of R-1 Tank.

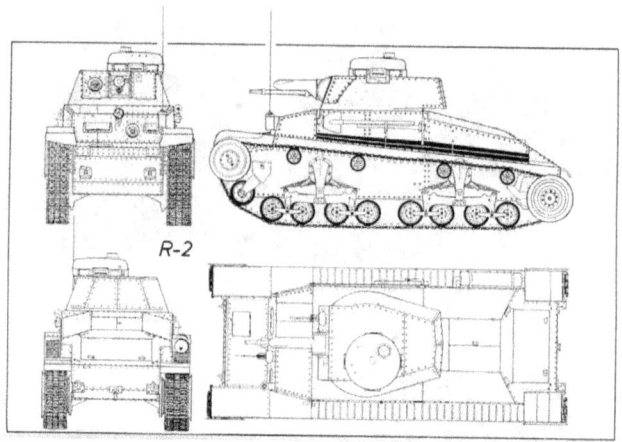

Technical profile of R-2 Tank.

Ion Antonescu and Adolf Hitler, Autumn 1940.

Although this restructuring at first glance may seem very appropriate, it really was not so much since these tanks were not acting as independent units but were divided between different infantry units (the crews of the tanks only received training to support to the infantry, following the outdated ideas that were acquired years ago copying the French). This was a real problem for the Romanian armored branch that would be very important during the war years, that determined that maximum performance would not be achieved. The main Romanian tanks at the beginning of the war were the R-2s and the R-35s. Both tanks were equipped with 37 mm guns, but to be honest, only the guns of the R-2 had some antitank capability, the R-35 guns were more suitable for use as infantry support guns (exactly what the Romanians wanted according to their obsolete military doctrine). Also the R-2s were better than the R-35s in speed and radio equipment, both elements very necessary if they wanted in some way to emulate the concept of the German *Blitzkrieg*. The Romanian political changes in 1940 were very important to understand the Romanian role during the first years of WWII. On September 6, 1940, King Carol II abdicated in favor of his son Mihail I. That same day, General and Prime Minister Ion Antonescu received unlimited powers acting from that moment as regent in the country.

A Parade of Romanian Troops.

Antonescu and Horia Sima.

General Ioan Sion.

Antonescu formed a new government in which included representatives of the Iron Guard or also called "*Legion of the Archangel Michael*" (nationalist group close to German ideas). After the visit on October 12 of a German military and diplomatic delegation, on November 23, 1940, beset by the situation of the country in Europe and internal political changes, Romania adhered to the Tripartite Pact. By then, the German military was already training the Romanian troops, as well as protecting the Romanian oil fields (which seemed necessary for the functioning of the German war machine, and which Hitler was willing to control directly).

Birth of the armored division

The WWII continued and Romania was still out of the conflict. But the increase in hostilities made the Romanian military high command realize that a remodeling of their armored forces was necessary, so that on April 17, 1941 the 1st Armored Division or *Divizia 1 blindata* was officially created (from the Motor-Mechanized Brigade whose denomination was changed). This unit, was constituted by the 1st and 2nd Tank Regiments, and the Vanatori 3rd and 4th Motorized Regiments. This Division was the most important unit in the Romanian Army and its history was very interesting because the several built and destructions of the *Divizia 1 blindata*. According to several sources, the Division had 283 officers, 433 non-commissioned officers, 6,014 soldiers, 5,367 rifles, 234 light machine guns, 39 heavy machine guns, 18 mortars, 36 artillery pieces, tanks (only 109 R-2 operational by early June 1941) and others 725 vehicles of several types. The Division was commanded by Brigadier General Ioan Sion (who would remain in office until January 10, 1942).

Romanian tanks on the Eastern front, 1941.

Romanian soldiers in combat, 1941.

Romanian R2 Czech *Škoda* LT-35 light tanks and *Škoda* H6ST6-T truck on the Eastern Front, 1941.

An important matter for the Romanian HQ about the Armored Division was that both tank types it had were very different in performance. So due to the great operational difference between the two main types of tanks used by the Romanians (the R-2 and the R-35), it was decided to leave the R-35 (and therefore the 2nd Tank Regiment) assigned to the 4th Army in infantry support tasks in the coming combats for Southern Bessarabia and Odessa.

For its part, the 1st Tank Regiment was inside the 1st Armored Division, becoming its only element constituted by battle tanks (this fact was the reason why during the 1941 campaigns, the 1st Armored Division would only use the R-2).

A Romanian tank R-2 in Bessarabia, 1941.

The Axis Forces

A Romanian R-35 tank in combat, Summer 1941.

A column of Romanian R-2 tanks marches down a street in Chisinau (Kishinev) in 1941. In the tank closest to the photographer you can see the Michael Cross painted on the engine compartment to facilitate aerial reconnaissance of Romanian tanks.

1st Division first blood

The war drums began to sound on the Eastern Front and troop movements were evident. In the spring of 1941, about 370000 German soldiers were stationed in Romania ready to attack the USSR. Despite the Romanian 1st Armored Division did not take part in the operation "*Barbarossa*" which started on June 22, 1941 by which it proceeded to the invasion of the USSR; although in a few days it would take part in the struggle against the Soviets (an attitude similar to the one of his Hungarian "allies", who declared war on the USSR on June 27). These allied countries were used in a second wawe against the Soviets, so the played at the beginning a secondary but important and neccesary role in the Eastern front.

During the 1941 campaign, the 1st Armored Division was used following the German military doctrine, that was as a shock unit against the enemy. This use obtained significant successes in the context of the battles for the conquest of Bessarabia (in the operation "*Munich*" for the capture of Bessarabia and Northern Bukovina, which took place after the "tranquility" in June and July when the front remained relatively static) and later in the Odessa siege between July and October 1941. The 1st Armored Division took part in the military operations carried out by Romania from almost the beginning of its intervention in the attack against the USSR, within the mixed German-Romanian formation constituted by the German XI Army and the 3rd and 4th Romanian Armies. On July 3, the Romanian Army crossed the Prut River and began an advance towards

in World War Two 1939-1945   57

Mogilev Podolski on Ukrainian lands. The 1st Armored Division crossed the Prut the same day and advanced towards Bratuseni-Edinita and did not have to wait long for the first Romanian tank battle against the Soviet tanks, which took place between July 4-5 in the vicinity of Brynzjena where a R-2 platoon clashed against 12 Soviet tanks that supported 74th and 176th Rifle Divisions troops (belonging to the 48th Rifle Corps). The result was the loss of an R-2 in exchange for the destruction of two T-28.

A destroyed soviet tank on the Prut Front, 1941.

Romanian Infantry in combat, 1941.

Ion Antonescu and King Michael I on the Eastern Front.

Romanian Anti-Tank Gun in combat, 1941.

From this moment, the next days were witness of continuous clashes against the Soviet troops that tried to resist the German steam-roller. The Romanian 1st Armored Division was then ordered to move southwards towards Mosana-Soroca (Soroki). From there on July 10, they managed to block retreating Soviet troops (from the 176th Rifle Division) heading towards Mogilev while clearing the right side of the Dnestr River in the Soroca area (Soroki). After that, they were subordinated to the 54th German Corps, with which on July 12 they participated in the capture of the town of Balti (Beltsy), to continue their harassment of the Soviets deployed in the town of Calarasi on July 14 where they lost 2 R-2 due to the Soviet artillery fire.

Romanian soldiers on the Eastern Front.

Chisinau: the Romanian army enters the city.

Romanian soldiers studying a map, August 1941.

There were a lot of clashes that we are not going to relate in this article due to its short extension. In all these combats, the tanks were used in small operative groups, which along with the deplorable lack of collaboration between Romanian tanks and infantry, caused very severe casualties in both men and material in the brand new 1st Armored Division. In the meantime the R-35s were supporting infatry troops in the Eastern front but very soon was evident (despite its powerful armor), that due to its low speed that in some cases they were prevented from taking part in mobile operations. This motivated that definitively the R-35 were relegated to a second place after the R-2.

The 1st Armored Division was forced to change its initial direction due to the heavy Soviet resistance, looking for operational zones with less difficult objectives, such as the capture of Chisináu (Kishinev) on July 16, 1941, which was done practically without enemy opposition (despite that, 1 R-2 was destroyed and 5 R-2 damaged). They continued their pressure against the enemy until they reached Tighina on July 19 (losing 3 R-2 during the clashes).

The campaign in Bessarabia finally ended on July 26, with the astonishing success of the Axis troops. The combat lead to the exhaustion to the Romanian Armored unit. The situation was so difficult, that the 1st Armored Division had to be out of service for ten days to try to put their vehicles in operational conditions again.

The Axis Forces

Portrait of a Romanian soldier, Summer 1941.

The Odessa siege

The Romanian people were happy with the result of the intervention of their Army in the conquest of Bessarabia, but this situation would change a few days later. On July 27, 1941, Hitler sent a letter to Antonescu, requesting Romanian collaboration for the capture of Odessa, in the Southern sector. On August 3, the 4th Romanian Army crossed the Dnestr River; on August 8, following Operational Directive No. 31, the Romanian High Command assigned the Romanian 4th Army the mission of defeating the Soviets between the Dnestr River and the Tiligulskiy area, and immediately afterwards headed for the city of Odessa. On the night between August 5 and 6, the Romanian 1st Armored Division crossed the Dnestr River, being subordinated to the Romanian V Corps fullfilling the mission of heading towards the Black Sea coast to attack the defenders of Odessa from the flank. Thanks to the tactical support of the armored vehicles, it was initially considered that Odessa (and its strategic port) would be captured in just a few days, despite being powerfully defended by the Soviets.

Romanian Cavalry Troops cross a bridge in the Eastern Front. The Romanian cavalry units had the support of the R-1 light tanks for armed reconnaissance tasks.

Romanian R-1 light tank Czech LT-34 captured by Soviet army in 1941 near Odessa.

An exhausted Romanian soldiers column advances through the inner of Odessa. Thanks to the bloody capture of the city in October 1941, Romania increased its prestige within the Axis.

Romanian soldiers fighting at Odessa.

Basically the assault on Odessa turned out to be a real carnage since three well-protected defensive lines plenty of fortifications had been built and planted with anti-tank trenches, machine gun places, pillboxes, etc; likewise, in order to harden the conditions further, lands had been flooded to make it more difficult for the Axis troops to enter the city. The Soviets really knew about the strategic importance of the city so they did their best in order to defend it. Detailing the arduous and painfully advance of the Romanian 1st Armored Division towards Odessa, on August 10 it managed to reach Bol.Buzhalyk (still in the first Soviet defensive line) expelling the Soviets from there. At sunset on the same day, the vanguard of the 1st Division managed to reach the second defensive line by Blagodatnaya - Mal.Adzhalyk; for shortly after to be reinforced with the troops of the 1st Romanian Cavalry Division. After a brief rest, between August 11 and 12 the 1st Armored Division continued its advance towards Gildendorf (Svitle), in the vicinity of the Kuyalnitsky estuary. In this area, in addition to the Soviet troops, heavy rains and mud caused that only in those two days, 13 Romanian tanks were out of service (although they could recover in a couple of days). As we can see, the advance was very hard for the Romanian tanks; and according to Axworthy and Cloutier the losses in the Romanian armored unit were distributed in this way: on August 11 they were out of combat 5 R-2, on the 12th they were 8 R-2, on August 13th 9 R-2 and on August 14th 25 R-2.

Romanian R-2 tank engaged in the Odessa siege.

A column of Romanian R-2 tanks, Summer 1941.

Odessa 1941: A Romanian *Schneider* anti tank gun.

Romanian Infantry take cover during an attack.

On August 18, the day was witnessed with multiple clashes between Romanians and Soviet defenders. Before dawn, Romanian troops supported by armored vehicles of the Romanian Armored Division 1st Regiment participated in the fighting for the Kagarlik, as well as for the capture of the Karpovo railway station.

Again, and continuing with the doctrine of the Romanian armored forces, the tanks did not act like an independent unit, but they were distributed between the troops of infantry to which they gave support and coverage. The fight was very heavy and in a single day the anti-tank fire from the enemy that managed to knock out 32 Romanian tanks (some of these tanks were recovered and repaired but only after a lot of time). In the so-called "*Karpovo disaster*", in addition to a large number of deaths, the Romanians in a single day had lost 35 R-2. The 1st Romanian Armored Division 1st Regiment had been left with only about 20 R-2 working (from 105 that it counted at the beginning of the combats in Odessa). Meanwhile the Romanian armored division 2nd Regiment with 74 obsolete R-35s, continued fighting for Odessa although with a very limited strategic value. The real fact is that since the last week of August 1941, out of more than 100 R-2 with which the Armored Division counted, there were only 20 in service (one Battalion). This situation was a great disaster for the Romanian Armor branch and for this reason it was decided on the 26th, that the remains of the 1st Armored Division were grouped in a formation called "*Lieutenant Colonel Eftimiu*" Mechanized Detachment. This unit only had about 20 R-2 (10 according to other sources, although less credible). Sadly the creation of little armored combat groups into the Romanian Army was very frecuent, but always due to the high losses in combat.

Romanian troops attacking, Summer 1941.

Romanian soldiers firing with a ZB-53.

A Romanian R-2 hit by the Soviet antitank artillery.

Romanian infantry in occupied Odessa, October 1941.

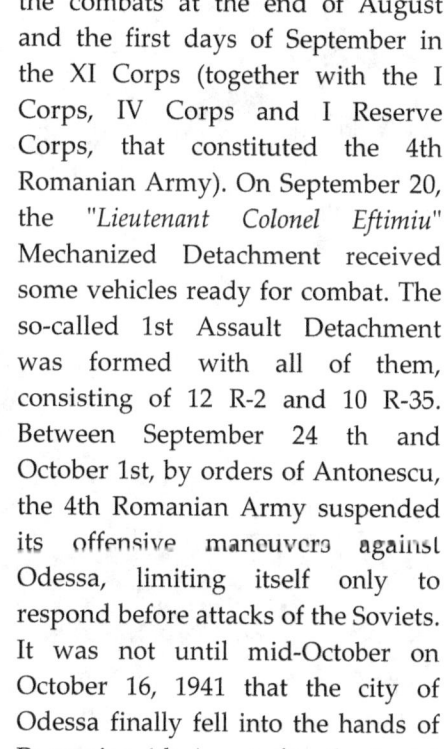

The "*Lieutenant Colonel Eftimiu*" Mechanized Detachment took part in the combats at the end of August and the first days of September in the XI Corps (together with the I Corps, IV Corps and I Reserve Corps, that constituted the 4th Romanian Army). On September 20, the "*Lieutenant Colonel Eftimiu*" Mechanized Detachment received some vehicles ready for combat. The so-called 1st Assault Detachment was formed with all of them, consisting of 12 R-2 and 10 R-35. Between September 24 th and October 1st, by orders of Antonescu, the 4th Romanian Army suspended its offensive maneuvers against Odessa, limiting itself only to respond before attacks of the Soviets. It was not until mid-October on October 16, 1941 that the city of Odessa finally fell into the hands of Romanian 4th Army after the Soviet defenders were evacuated (mainly because of the inability of the Soviets to keep the city in their hands) thanks to the intervention of Soviet Navy. At the end of October 1941, the 1st Armored Division was in a very bad situation so it became necessary to transfer it to Romania in order to be repaired, resupplied, re-trained and reorganized (it needed more than 10 months to reacquire combat capacity again).

A Parade of Romanian armored troops in Odessa, October 1941.

A Romanian T-3 tank (*PzKpfw.III Ausf. N*) on the Eastern Front, Autumn 1942.

A Romanian T-4 tank (*PzKpfw.IV Ausf. G*) moves through the field. The arrival of more than 100 tanks of this type, allowed the Romanian 1st Armored Division and some other units to significantly increase their firepower.

1942. The rebuilding and destroying of the armored division

The participation of Romanian armor was conspicuous by its absence during the first half of 1942. It was decided that the rest of the 1st Armored Division along with some other units also rebuilt were assigned to the 3rd Romanian Army in its advance through the southern USSR. It was necessary to wait until September 1942 when the 1st Armored Division transferred to the Eastern Front, although the 1st Armored Division was not be operational again until October 17, 1942; it was finally reorganized thanks to the incorporation of new armored material from Germany. These tanks were from types more powerful to any tank type that Romania had put until that moment in service; we refer to 11 Pz.III N (in Romania as T3) and to 11 Pz. IV G (now referred to as T4).

A Russian T-26 captured by Romanian soldiers.

A Romanian anti tank gun on the Eastern Front, 1942.

Romanian soldiers on the Eastern Front, 1942.

Stalingrad. The annihilation of 1st Armored Division.

In November 19, only 19 of the 22 tanks were available, although it is true that a copy of the T-3 and another of the T-4 were sent to Romania to be dedicated to training new crews in these new tanks). According to Axworthy, at that time the Division had 2 Soviet tanks captured in service (the first with 7 tons and the second one with 12 tons). The Romanian unit was also reinforced with the necessary artillery guns to enhance its anti-tank capacity, with 9 50 mm Pak 38 and 9 75 mm Pak 40 with their corresponding *Zugkraftwagen* tractors. Finally the motorized Division reconnaissance troops were strengthened with several armored vehicles *Sdkfz 222* (6) and *Sdkfz 223* (5). They were attached to Army Group B commanded by Marshal von Bock, the 4th Panzer Army, part of the 2nd Hungarian Army, the 2nd and 6th German Armies and the 3rd Romanian Army; with the mission to support the left wing of the German advance towards Stalingrad. The operational force available to the Division just before the operations aimed at the Stalingrad takeover were initiated was as follows:

- 501 officers.
- 538 NCOs.
- 11,592 soldiers.
- 9,335 rifles.
- 278 light machine guns.
- 61 heavy machine guns.

- 67 mortars.
- 36 cannons and howitzers.
- 1,358 vehicles.
- 109 R-2.
- 11 T-3.
- 11 T-4.
- 2 captured Soviet tanks (possibly a T-60 and a BT-7).
- 10 AB armored vehicles (Sdkfz 222). Posibly adquired after Soviet attack started.
- 8 armored personnel carriers (SPW 251). Posibly adquired after Soviet attack started.

The Division was subordinated to the 48th German Panzer Corps (under the command of Lieutenant General Ferdinand Heim) as were the 22nd German Panzer Division and parts of the 14th Panzer Division. On October 9 the Romanian Armored Division joined the 6th German Army near Chernychevska, which was already preparing for the assault on the city of Stalingrad; leaving the Division subordinated to the 48th German Panzer Corps.

The training of the crews of the newcomers T-3 and T-4 within the 1st Armored Division could not be very good since by mid-November 1942 the Soviets would carry out a counter-offensive that would end the training. Immediately before the Soviet offensive, the 1st Armored Division was in the vicinity of Perelazovskij and Petrovka to cross the Chir River and had service at 84 R-2, 19 T3 and T4 and two captured Soviet tanks.

The distribution within the 1st Armored Division was in three Combat Groups:

"Coronel Pastia" Group, *"Coronel Nistor"* Group and *"Otto Benedict"* Reconnaissance Group.

Romanian troops near Don area, 1942.

A R-1 tank 8th Cavalry Division.

Romanians fighting on the Don, 1942.

Russian tank crew surrendering to Romanian soldiers, Eastern Front, Summer 1942.

A Romanian R-2 tank belonging to the 1st Armored Division drives over a snowered terrain at Stalingrad Front, Autumn 1942.

On November 19, 1942 when the Soviets began their winter offensive (Operation Uranus), the 3rd Romanian Army had 152492 Romanians and 11211 Germans. The enemies arranged against the Romanian 3rd Army were the Soviet South-Western Front, composed of the 1st Guard Army, 5th Armored Army and the 21st Army. This Soviet South-Western Front had 728 tanks, 790 aircraft and 5888 artillery pieces.

The 48th Panzer Corps commander, at 5.50 am, was aware of the massive Soviet attack, and ordered that reconnaissance missions be carried out in the Kletskaya and Bolshoyie areas. He knew about the difficult situation of his troops because the Soviets had a lot of soldiers and tanks. After receiving the reports from his reconnaissance troops and without any specific authorization from the Army Group HQ, he decided to send the 48th Panzer Corps northeast to stop the Soviet advance on Kletskaia with a counterattack. So at 10.00 AM the order was given for the 1st Romanian Armored Division and the 22nd Panzer Division (and a Kampfgruppe Group belonging to the 14th Panzer Division) to head towards Kletskaia, along with the 7th Cavalry Division to try to tackle the Soviet onslaught. But the confusion, together with the hesitant orders from Adolf Hitler, determined that at 11.30 AM, the Romanian and German armored units were redirected to the northwest. Although the massive Red Army was the winner indeed before its start, the Axis troop reaction was so slow that the only way for them was resist and try to fly to other defensive line deep inside, but only part of the Axis troops achieved their goal. On the first day of the offensive, the enemy succeeded in creating two breaches in the defensive line of the 3rd Romanian Army. One located in the center of the lines of the 3rd Romanian Army, with 16-18 kilometers in width and with a depth of 15 kilometers, being the other breach achieved in the right wing (between the 3rd Romanian Army and the 6th German Army) with 10-12 kilometers wide with a depth of 35-40 kilometers. During the first day of the offensive, casualties on both sides were very high in human lives and in battle tanks (62 lost by the Soviets at the hands of the Romanians, while the Romanians themselves lost 25 of their own tanks).

The weather conditions in which the Romanian soldiers met during the winter in USSR were hard, as can be seen in these photographs.

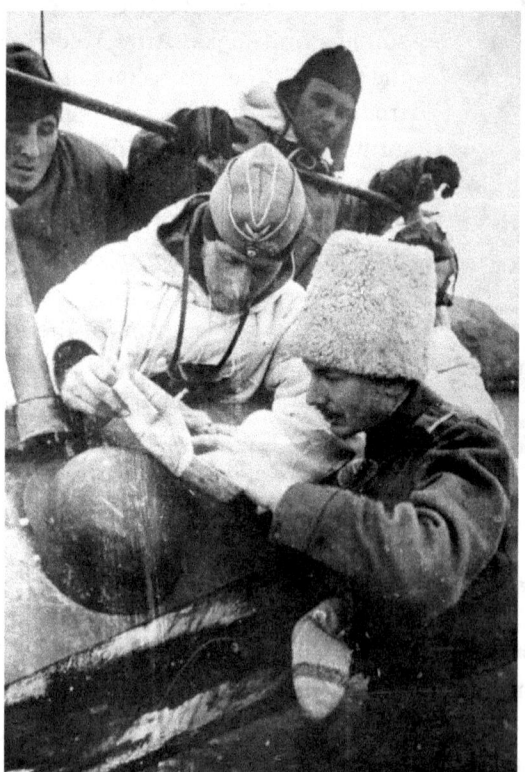

German and Romanian officers, Autumn 1942.

During day 20, one of the most important fights in which the Romanian 1st Armored Division was involved was the counterattack against the Winterlager farm. This farm was in the path that the Romanian division had to follow to try to connect with the 22nd German Panzer Division and it was already occupied by important Soviet forces that became strong in the position. During this Romanian action there were several Romanian tankers who in their Pz.IIIs and Pz.35(t)s risked their lives in continuous attacks until they finally managed to break the resistance of the defenders. But that small success was continued by a massive Soviet counterattack with tanks at dusk so the Romanian tanks fought until they ran out of ammunition then they flied. For its part, the Romanian 3rd Army at the end of day 20, had a hole in the center of its defensive line over 70 kilometers wide; immediately behind this fracture in the Romanian lines, the Romanian 1st Armored Division was encircled. The 5th, 6th and 15th Infantry Divisions, as well as remnants of the 13th and 14th Infantry Divisions, were also surrounded very fast. In total the infantry troops in the pocket were some 40,000 men, who formed the so-called *"General Lascar"* Combat Group. For this reason, the Romanian 1st Armored Division (which was in the Nishne Zaritzya area) that was the most powerful unit in the pocket was entrusted with the mission of fighting south-southwest towards the Perelasovski to cover the left flank of the 5th Division Infantry that was in the western heights in the Zaritzya valley.

Stalingrad Front 1942: three Romanian soldiers using a ZB-30 7.92 mm light machine gun.

Mounted Russian Infantry ride T-34's into battle.

A Romanian *PzKpfw.III* on the Stalingrad Front, 1942.

The battle went on and from the dawn November 22, the 1st Romanian Armored Division separated definitively from the rest of the Combat Group *"General Lascar"* units that remained behind, while it continued advancing slowly towards Bol.Donschynka. The slow advance of the non motorized Romanian troops condemned them to be left behind with the high risk of be smashed by the Soviets. In their march towards the south, on November 22 near of the town of Bol.Donschynka In their flying way, the 1st Romanian Armored Division found a Soviet cavalry unit (possibly belonging to the 8th Soviet Cavalry Corps) that had the support of armored T-60 and T-70 tanks. The 112th Soviet Cavalry Division attacked near Bol.Donschynka against Romanian infantry troops supported by some 25 tanks belonging to the Romanian 1st Armored Division. In these combats the tanks belonging to 1st Armored Regiment 7th Company did their work successfully, because they finally defeated their rivals without backing off their positions in Bol.Donschynka.

Romanian soldiers at Don's Bend 1942.

A column of Soviet tanks.

December 1942. A column of Romanian prisoners.

On November 23, the 1st Armored Division was quite depleted in its potential, since it had only 19 R-2, 11 T-3 and T-4 working (some other tanks that were damaged or without fuel, were under tow); and these were generally quite damaged and short of fuel again.

But they didn't stop so on the 25th the Romanian armored troops managed to cross the river Chir by the bridge in Gussinka.

After the protection of the Chir River defensive line, the remains of the 1st Romanian Armored Division (only 5 tanks R-2 and 1 T-3 working) had managed to reach the "security" by crossing the Chir River.

On December 2, the Romanian 1st Armored Division had only two tanks in service and about 944 men of the initial 12,000; so it can practically be considered that its usefulness at the front was zero.

Disaster on the Stalingrad Front, December 1942.

1943. Reorganization after the disaster

The Romanian Army lost 158854 men wounded, dead and missing during the Stalingrad campaign from November 19, 1942 to January 7, 1943, which represented almost half of the Romanian Army. The Romanian 1st Armored Division suffered a very high number of casualties in both men and vehicles. The tanks that were in the process of repair at the beginning of the year 1943 were 54 F-17, 2 T-4, 2 T-3, 25 R-2 and 52 R-35. The Romanian Armored Division destruction degree was such that it was in the process of reconstruction relegated to training tasks, and would not be operational until August 1944. It was in March 1943, when the 50 T-38s were handed out to the Romanians from Germans. These tanks were first sent to the Crimea, where in June 1943 the Romanian crews were trained in their new tanks. On November 30, 15 T-38 of the 51st Armored Company were repatriated to Romania. On December 12, 5 T-38 from the 52nd Company were sent to Romania. In December, the T-38 that remained operative to *Batalionul care da lupta T-38* were only 10, which finally would be sent to Romania at the beginning of 1944. In the autumn of 1943, Romanians finally managed to get one of their requests for new non-obsolete armored material accepted by Germany. Following the guidelines of the Olivenbaum Program (on September 23, 1943 the Germans agreed to carry out the armored delivery program called Olivenbaum I, which should be followed by the II and III), they proceeded to the sale of armored material between the months of November 1943 and July 1944. The vehicles that were sold were 114 tanks Pz.Kpfw IV (most of the tanks were Pz.IVH, but there were some F-2 and J), 98 StuG III (assault guns), and 2 BefPz.Wg IV (command

Two TACAM T-60 during a parade on May 1943.

Various Romanian T-38 in Crimea during 1943, where they were integrated into the *Batalionul care de lupta T-38*, divided in three Companies.

Some Romanian Pz.IV tank on the Eastern Front.

vehicles based on Pz. IV, of which 3 copies had been promised). At last, the Romanian armored troops could use modern tanks against their Soviet enemies.

1944. Between the Sword and the Wall

The advance of the Soviets during 1944 was constantly maintained on all fronts. Romanian armored formations were needed at the front, but the 1st Armored Division was still in full reorganization period. An emergency solution had to be found, which consisted on creating a partially armored unit, which could be sent to the front. So, on February 24, the so-called Grupului Mixt Care of Luptă or "*Cantemir*" Mixed Armored Group in Northern Transnitria was created. It was in the Moldovan front where the 1st Armored Division finally went back and on April 28 1944 it was named "*Romania Mare*" or "Great Romania" (in English) a resemblance of the German Grossdeutschland Division. The withdrawal of the German troops during 1944 before the Soviet push had delayed them to the borders of Romania before the war, although at least they managed to establish a defensive line along the Dniester River called the Trajan Line except for two bridgeheads that the Soviets had managed to establish. In a few days, the Axis troops realized that their defensive lines was very weak in order to stop the Soviet attack. The overall equipment of the "*Romania Mare*" was not complete when the Soviet offensive took place so that on August 19 1944 it had the following armored vehicles: 48 T-4s (Pz. IVH), 12 TAs (StuG III Ausf.G), 24 TBs armored transports (SPW 250 or 251) and 12 ABs armored vehicles (Sdkfz 222). In addition, the 1st Armored Division had under its command a German unit, the "Major Brausch" Detachment. This unit was formed by a Company with 10 StuG IIIs and a Motorized Infantry Battalion. Finally, the attack for the invasion of Romania was shared by 2 Soviet Fronts coordinated by Marshal Timoshenko, who were deployed along a frontline of about 400 kilometers:

German and Romanian officers reviewing a map southern Ukraine, April 1944.

Romanian soldier with a *panzerschreck*.

Several Romanian soldiers traveling in a SPW in the Transylvanian Front after the change of side of Romania in August 1944.

A Romanian R-1 light tank marching, 1944.

A German *Panther* on the Romanian Front, 1944.

-3rd Ukrainian Front: commanded by Marshal Fyodor Tolbukhin and deployed in the left front area next to the Black Sea.

-2nd Ukrainian Front: commanded by Marshal Rodion Yakovlevich Malinovsky and deployed on the right side of the Soviet attack front.

At night, on August 19-20, in prevention against an upcoming Soviet attack, the 1st Armored Division headed towards Goesti, Crucea and Sinesti, about 10-14 kilometers southeast of Podu Iloaiei. Inevitably, when the powerful Soviet attack was unleashed, the defensive line was broken in the Bahlui valley, between the towns of Baltati and Letcani. It is important to keep in mind that the *"Romania Mare"* was not deployed as an only Unit in the same location, but was deployed in different combat groups that weakened the Romanian Armored Division strength: on the one hand the 1st Tank Regiment, on the other hand the 3rd Regiment Motorized Vanatori (reinforced with the 1st Assault Tank Company 1st Tank Regiment commanded by slt. Constantinescu) and finally the 4th Vanatori Motorized Regiment (reinforced by the 3rd Assault Tank Company 1st Tank Regiment commanded by Captain Grabinski). It was around 10 am when the Romanian vanguard met with a formation of tanks belonging to the Soviet vanguard one kilometer south of Scobalteni. But the surprise for the Romanians was that they were not facing a flank of the Soviet approach, instead, they came up against the Soviet approach line. The battle for Scobalteni of the 1st Tank Regiment had lasted for about ten hours, causing both sides a large number of casualties. In fact, it is estimated that some 34 armored vehicles (between T-4 and TA) had been lost by the Romanians at nightfall on the 20th.

A column of German *'Panther'* tanks belonging to the *'Grossdeutschland'* Division advancing along a road in poor condition on the Romanian Front in April 1944.

Soviet troops cheered on the streets of Bucharest on August 31, 1944.

An MG team firing a ZB-53 machinegun, October 1944.

Faced with the accomplished facts and the success of the Soviet breakthrough, Hitler had to authorize the withdrawal towards the Focsani-Namaloasa-Braila line or FNB (what Antonescu had requested on repeated occasions during that summer of 1944); although, as the events showed, it was too late for that.

On the afternoon on August 23, Conducator Ion Antonescu was arrested along with two of his ministers; for a short while later King Michael I solemnly announced on a radio transmission the formation of a new Government under the command of Constantin Sănătescu (who had been until January 1944 the commander-in-chief of the 4th Army). In addition, the end of the fighting was announced in Romania when all the troops received the order to stop the fight (at 00.30 am on August 24 the Romanian divisions belonging to the 4th Army formally received the cease-fire order with the Soviets); while negotiators were sent to the Soviet Union and to the Soviet commanders from the units that were in front of the Romanians troops. The withdrawal of the Romanian armor continued. The Romanian 1st Tank Regiment armored column, already knowing the news of the armistice, continued its advance towards the south, seeking shelter within its own country.

In the foreground several Romanian SPW 251 are heading toward the front line, Summer 1944.

Two Romanian gunners prepare to fire.

A Romanian soldier with *Panzerfaust*.

The Romanian military only had two alternatives (despite many attempts by the Romanian authorities to avoid both), either surrender and be turned into prisoners or in some cases join to Soviet units and fight under their command against their former allies. These men were not interned, since for some of them the war was not over, their fate was the formation of the armored Detachment "*Lt. Col. Gheorghe Matei*". The total number of the new group was of 1058 men and of 133 different types vehicles, that were assigned to the Soviet 7th Guard Army; the 1st Tank Regiment was officially dissolved because of the wishing of the Soviets (they could not allow important Romanian units that worked independent from their new "Soviet friends"). Almost simultaneously, at the Târgoviste Army Mechanized Training Center (with vehicles from the same center), a new unit was created under the protection of the Soviets. It was the "*General Nicolescu*" Armored Detachment (also known as "*Jupiter*"). In fact, to further increase control over the Romanian armor, the "*General Nicolescu*" Armored Detachment and the "*Lt. Col. Gheorghe Matei*" Armored Detachment were merged a short time later in a new formation: the 4th Army's Armored Group. A third formation that the Soviets authorized to build was the "*Mr. Victor Popescu*" Armored Detachment which was made of men and vehicles from the 1st Armored Training Division. As far as the end of 1944, only the 2nd Tank Regiment remained active as an armored unit, which was constituted by:

- 1st tank battalion: with a tank company with 8 T-4s and a company of assault guns with 13 TAs.

- 2nd Battalion of tanks (light): with two Tank Companies with 28 R-35s and R-35/45s, a Tank Company T-38 with 9 units and a TACAM Battery with 5 TACAM R-2s.

One of the few existing photographs of a Romanian TA assault gun in April 1945 during the clashes in Moravia. This TA belonged to the 2nd Tank Regiment (*Regimentului 2 Care of Luptă*) and shows the insignia of the star in a white circle.

1945. Fight until the end and annihilation

The Soviet HQ had decided that the Romanian units that were fighting within the Soviet Army had to be used until their annihilation, because if the post war Romania was weak, the possibility of any revolt against the USSR was almost non-existent. So, the Romanian 2nd Tank Regiment would be assigned to the Soviet 27th Guard Armored Corps in March 1945, being under the command of this unit. The first destination of his journey against the Axis was Slovakia, where the 2nd Romanian Tank Regiment was sent in February 1945, to be later sent to the front line and assigned to the 27th Armored Corps of the Soviet Guard in March. Between March 25 and May 5, 1945, the Romanian armored troops continued its participation in the war in the Soviet offensive by the capture of Bratislava and Brno with the troops of the 2nd Ukrainian Front commanded by Marshal Malinovsky. During the battles between February and May 1945, the Romanian 2nd Tank Regiment was first in Czechoslovakia, then in Austria and finally again in Czechoslovakia, the Romanian armored group fought almost continuously demonstrating high fighting spirit. They had only one option, and it was to fight alongside the Soviet Army until the end of the war and try to survive. But, the Romanian had no time to rest nor replenish or repair their armament and vehicles. In just a couple of months of fighting the casualties reached 93% of the armored vehicles (only one T-4 survived the fighting in service conditions). Having always demonstrated great value in the combat line, the Soviets did not want to allow the Romanian 2nd Tank Regiment to continue to exist after the end of World War II, forcing the Romanians to hand over the few armored vehicles that were still in service and later they dissolved the Romanian 2nd Tank Regiment.

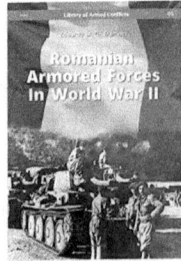

Thanks to Kagero Publishers for allow to publish this article based in *"Romanian Armored Forces in World War II"* book in this magazine.

Bibliography
Mark Axworthy, "*The Romanian Army of World War II*", Osprey Publishing

Mark Axworthy, "*Third Axis Fourth Ally: Romanian Armed Forces in the European War, 1941-1945*", Arms & Armour

E.M. Gil Martinez, "*Romanian Armored Forces In World War II*", Kagero Publishing

The Axis Forces

in World War Two 1939-1945

www.ingramcontent.com/pod-product-compliance
Lightning Source LLC
LaVergne TN
LVHW081546070526
838199LV00057B/3795